Purple
Heaven
And Other Stories

Purple Heaven

And Other Stories

by John Madison Culler

Illustrations by Anderson Riley, Jr.

JOHN CULLER & SONS
CAMDEN, SOUTH CAROLINA

DESIGNED BY WENDY L. TRUBIA
ILLUSTRATIONS BY ANDERSON RILEY, JR.

ISBN 1-887269-01-0

JOHN CULLER & SONS
P.O. BOX 1277
CAMDEN, SOUTH CAROLINA 29020
1-800-861-9188

Dedication...

To my wife of 39 years, Linda (Sweet Dreams) Culler,
the queen of the wind, who never knew what was
coming next, but always handled it with a smile,
whatever it was.

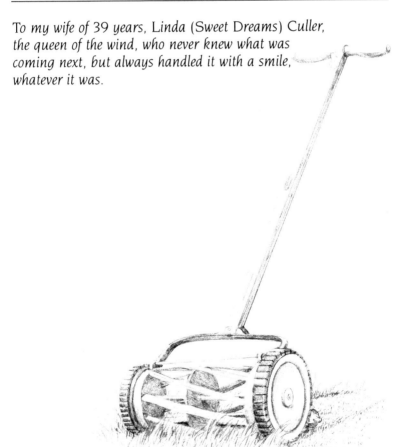

Blame...

Blame this book on Chap Jackson of Birmingham,
Alabama. He is a no-account, low-down bait
fisherman and nighthunter who bugged me for
ten years to publish it. He expects his copy free.

Contents

Purple Heaven

*It's not easy, planning what you
want to do for forever, and like the
old saying, you better be careful what
you wish for... you just might get it!*

I died and went to heaven. At least, that's what my ticket said. I noticed it was stamped in purple though, and everyone else with a heaven ticket had theirs stamped in gold. I really didn't want to say much about it, seeing as how there was a fair amount of groaning and gnashing of teeth from those who had a ticket to another place, so I kept quiet and shuffled to the gate that said, "Heaven, Purple."

There were long lines in front of the other two gates, but when I got to mine I was the only one there. While I waited I thought back over my life and wondered why I hadn't gone straight to hell, because that was what I had been working for. Besides, everyone I knew would be there. Occasionally, though, at times during my life I had been lucky. Evidently this was one of those times.

Presently a very dignified gentleman with a white robe and a long white beard opened the other heaven gate and with much fanfare welcomed each of the folks in the other line. He gave all of them a brochure, (four color, accordion fold) describing

their new life and the rewards they had earned. Several of the fortunate souls had opened their brochures before they passed me and were having trouble folding them up again. Must be printed by the Heaven Highway Department, I reasoned.

No sooner was that bunch out of sight than around the corner came a fellow with rhythm in his step wearing a green leisure suit and carrying a big key. He was singing "Whiskey, Women and Loaded Dice," under his breath, and when he passed he winked at me.

"Howdy, podner," I said, hoping he would think I was from Texas. I always wanted to be first in something, and I figured I might as well be the first Texan to go to heaven. I don't think I fooled him, because he bopped on down and opened the gate for that crowd who were gnashing their teeth. They didn't go through the gate with nearly the enthusiasm the first bunch did, 'cause there was all that weeping and wailing, but go they did, and soon I was the only one left.

I waited and waited, but no one came. Hours passed. I started to leave several times, but didn't know anywhere else I could go. I had never heard of but two places for those who were lately departed, besides the other gates were locked. Finally, I heard footsteps on the other side of the fence, and a black guy with a bounce in his step came into view. He was wearing a beige silk suit, a Panama hat, and was smoking a fat Tampa Nugget.

"Afternoon, podner," he grinned, showing off his gold fillings.

"You must be from Texas," I asked.

"Nope, Charleston. Least, that's in my other life. I've moved up considerable."

He unlocked the gate and I stepped through. "Welcome to Purple Heaven," he said. "By the looks of your record, you sure do deserve it."

"Who are you?" I asked, but I wasn't real sure I wanted to know.

"I'm Saint Leroy," he confessed. I told him I had heard of a few saints, but until now, had never heard of him. He said he wasn't surprised, since the record showed I was not only real slow, but at times entirely blank.

I followed him down the walk, out of the building and into a little patch of fog about knee-high. He snapped his fingers, everything began spinning around, and suddenly we were standing on a dirt road in front of an old country store. A big sign on the front read, "Drink Coca-Cola," and under it, "Purple Heaven."

"All right now," he said as he took a little book out of his pocket. "What do you want to do?" That question took me by surprise; I never thought you would have to tell them that sort of stuff when you got to heaven. Besides, I had no idea just how good I could make old Purple Heaven.

"I like to shoot ducks," I ventured rather timidly. This seemed to be all right with him, and he wrote it down. He asked me if I preferred any particular kind of duck, and I told him greenheads. Big mallets. He wrote that down too, and waited. I figured that was my cue, and I told him I had always wanted to catch a world record largemouth bass.

"How big is that?" He sure didn't know much to be a saint.

"Twenty-two pounds, four ounces," I said, "but twenty pounds will be o.k. iffen you ain't got a real big one." He said not to worry about it.

"What do you like to eat?" That was an easy one. Fried pork chops and fresh collards and ice tea with one of them lemon squeezers. He wrote it down. Oh yes, and cornbread

"Anything else?"

He seemed willing enough, but I didn't want to be greedy. After all, a fellow stays dead a long, long time. I figured I had plenty of time later for other stuff.

"How about some female company?" he suggested. I hadn't thought of that. "After all, you will be the only one around, and we've got some mighty beautiful girls up here."

I decided to shoot for the moon. "I want Marilyn Monroe and Jayne Mansfield," I said. He nodded, and wrote it down. I was on a roll. "And I don't just want 'em here, I want 'em warm and willing, like in that country song!"

"You got it," he grinned. "You want them both at one time?" I told him I didn't, I wanted them to share me, half and half.

He asked if I could think of anything else I could possibly want, because, after all, "this is Purple Heaven, and you get what you want." I couldn't think of another thing.

"All right," he said, putting his book in his hip pocket. "That store is where you get all your gear and shells and stuff, ain't nobody in there, just help yourself."

"Where do I sleep?" I asked, 'cause I didn't see anything but the store and a small lake off in the distance.

"Sleep?" He looked like I had poured out his Jack Daniels. "Man, this is heaven! Don't nobody sleep in heaven!" He went on to explain that there was an apartment on top of the store where I could be alone with the girls; that I would take my meals under the big shade tree next to the store, and I was to shoot ducks and fish in the pond.

If I wanted him, he said, I was to ring a big brass bell on a post next to the tree. I was anxious to get to it, but the weather was about seventy degrees and clear, so I figured it must be Spring. I asked the saint when duck season came in heaven, and was told it stayed in all year and there was no bag limit.

"Boy," I thought, "this is one *fine* place."

Far as I could tell, I was the only lucky soul in Purple Heaven. There wasn't anyone in the store, on the street or anywhere. I went on in the store and grabbed a couple of boxes of shells, a pair of waders, and after a few agonizing minutes at the gun rack, a premium grade Model 12, still in the box but made in 1960.

When I walked out on the porch a big black Labrador retriever was sitting there. "An extra added plus," I thought. Old Purple Heaven was going to be jam up and jelly tight!

We walked down to the pond, the sun was shining brightly, the weather was warm, and it was really nice to be out, but I didn't have much hope for the duck situation. There was only one blind, so we walked in, sat down and I began to load my gun. Suddenly, a brace of mallards came directly over the blind, and I jumped up and scored the neatest double you ever saw. "The old boy still has it when it counts," I thought to myself, and felt rather pleased. The dog executed perfectly. Both ducks, laid neatly side by side in the bottom of the blind. One thing peculiar though – – he never shook off. I was used to having an ice water shower after a retriever got back to the blind, but no matter.

Suddenly a loner drake came over, and I nailed him on the first shot. Another perfect retrieve. Two more came by, and I scored another double. Five in a row! You are not gonna believe this, but I shot ducks that afternoon until I began to feel ashamed of myself, and never missed a single one! I knew I was good, but I never really knew just how fantastic I was until that afternoon. I must have killed a hundred big greenheads, never missed a shot, and the dog retrieved each one perfectly. That son-of-a-gun even laid them ten to a row!

I wasn't tired, but I didn't want to kill all the ducks in Purple Heaven the first day, so I put the ducks in some old sacks I found in the blind and walked back to the store. If the fishing is as good here as the duck hunting, this is gonna be some kind of great place, I thought as I picked up a casting rod and selected some plugs at the store. They sure had a lot of plugs, so it wasn't easy. There was a small boat and a paddle in the pond, so I went down to see if I could raise anything.

Again, you ain't gonna believe this, but on the first cast I got a mighty strike, and finally put the biggest bass I had ever seen in the boat. I didn't know bass grew that big. My heart was pounding and I was really excited, but when on my second cast I caught another just like the first, I almost passed out. It was too much to believe.

Yep, it got better and better. I must have cast fifty more times, and caught fifty more of the same whopper bass. After I loaded the little boat down with world record bass, I was in danger of sinking and had to paddle in. I dragged the bass up to the store and weighed them – – you guessed it! Each one weighed twenty-two pounds, four ounces. Fifty world record tying bass on fifty casts. I figured I must have been the world's greatest bass fisherman all along, I just needed a good place to fish.

By now I was getting a tad hungry, so I walked out under the tree. The table was all set with fried pork chops, a big bowl of collards, a cast iron skillet of cornbread and a gallon or two of ice tea. Talkin' 'bout good! Whoever cooked that meal sure knew how to run a store.

I was just about finished when I heard someone calling my name. I looked around, and there was Marilyn, up on the second floor of the store, calling me and giggling. She was even more beautiful than in the movies. I'm telling you I finished up those pork chops fast and headed for the stairs. Marilyn was everything I had hoped she'd be and even more. What made it so great, she thought I was the greatest lover that had ever lived!

After about two hours with Marilyn, I got to thinking about those ducks again, so I picked up some more shells, whistled up the dog, and headed for the pond. It happened again. One hundred shots, one hundred clean kills, one hundred flawless

15

retrieves. It was the way heaven oughta be!

I took the ducks up to the store, picked up my fishing gear and – – you ain't gonna believe this – – caught fifty more world record bass on fifty casts! All on a frog pattern Dalton Special!

All that excitement molded something of an appetite, so I went out under the tree and there it was again – – pork chops, collards, cornbread and ice tea, with a lemon squirter. Let me tell you that was livin' high on the hog! Just about the time I finished up, I heard my name being called, and when I looked up, it was Jayne up in the window – – the shift had changed!

Up the stairs I went, and I'm here to tell you that girl was some kinda fine! And boy, was she glad to see me! But the most amazing thing was, she thought I was the greatest lover she had ever seen!

Purple Heaven had a crazy old sun that went neither up nor down, but just sorta' floated around in the sky. Made it hard to tell if you were eating supper or breakfast. Since I didn't have to sleep, 'cause I never got tired, I figured it didn't really matter much, so I got the gun and dog and shot more ducks. After that I caught some more world record bass. After that I ate some more pork chops and collards. Then it was Marilyn's turn to be the lucky girl. And so on.

Weeks went by. At least they would have if that crazy sun had acted right. I stayed full time killin' ducks, catching bass, eating collards, chops and cornbead and making love to those beautiful, lucky, lucky girls. I drank enough tea to flood hell.

Before long I noticed a funny thing about those two girls. They were warm and willin' all right, which is what I wanted, but that's all they wanted to do. I couldn't even talk to them

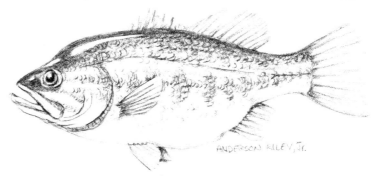

ANDERSON RILEY, Jr.

16

without they would try to put their arms around my neck. Now I know I was handsome and charming, but it looked like to me they would want to play cards or something sometime, or even wash the dishes. They didn't. I even thought of a joke once and had to tell it to myself because they wouldn't have appreciated it. However, as you might imagine, it wasn't very funny that way.

Then a weird thing started happening down at the duck pond. I would sorta point the gun in the direction of the duck and shoot, and he would fall dead. That was fun for awhile. I aimed at the bottom of the blind and killed a single off to the right. I aimed right between that unemotional dog's eyes and dropped the last bird in a flight of three passing over. Finally, showing the cold nerve of a burglar, I stuck the gun in my britches and touched her off. Dropped a drake quartering away.

The same thing happened fishing. Good cast or bad had the same result – – a world record bass. I even stood up in the boat, took the Dalton Special in my hand and flung it down as hard as I could in the water. Right – – another record bass.

Even the pork chops and collards were wearing a little thin. Got to where I couldn't eat but half of 'em. But the girls were the worst. Seems like every other minute one of them was calling me, and she didn't have but one thing on her mind. They didn't want to go hunting, they didn't want to go fishing, they didn't want to sit on the porch and rock, all they wanted was me! Day and night, noontime too!

Things weren't working out exactly right. I rang the bell and called the saint.

When he came, I explained I appreciated being there and all, and I knew they must have worked awful hard to get it set up, but that things weren't working out.

He said I should be ashamed of myself, that there were literally millions of guys who would swap places with me in a minute, and that I should relax and enjoy Purple Heaven. "After all," he said, "you've earned it."

So I gave it another try. For about a month. I got to where I would just sit under the tree and shoot fifty times, and the dog would go down to the lake and bring the ducks up to the store and stack 'em up. After awhile I would shoot and then try to knock the dog in the head with the gun when he ran by. Never did. He was a quick little bugger.

Ducks, bass, porkchops and making love. Ducks, bass, porkchops and making love. It never stopped. I swore that if I ever saw another buxom blonde I was gonna barf on my shoes!

Got to where I would climb the tree and try to hide. They found me every time. It was the worst kind of hell you can imagine!

I rang the bell.

"Listen, you haint, I've had it with this junk. I want to go hunting sometime when I don't kill nothing and fishing when I can't get a strike. I want to get dog tired and go to sleep and wake up and find something here beside these confounded collards! And I want a woman who laughs at my jokes and has headaches and ain't in the mood so cotton pickin' much! And I want a dog that shakes water on me and stinks and can't find the birds half the time!"

He gave me the fish eye. "You mean you want to leave this place? This place that has everything you wanted?"

"Right. On the first fog out."

"You say that one more time and I'm taking you up on the offer, you ungrateful heathen. I'll send you back to earth so fast won't anyone even know you've been gone."

"Say goodby to the girls, for me, haintface."

All of a sudden I'm sitting in my front porch swing. My wife is calling. "John! I told you to come in here and take this garbage out!"

Thank God!

the Jumping *off* Place

*When your dreams run out of gas you might
feel a powerful tug to show up here, but it isn't
like it used to be. Now you have a chance to be
something other than a shooting star.*

My friend Dave seemed to know what he was talking about when he gave me directions, but I didn't trust my memory so I made him draw me a map. You know how it is when you go somewhere new, you just don't want to fool around.

Dave had been promising for two or three years to tell me how to get to what he described as the "number one bass pond in the world" but up until now he always managed to find an excuse. I don't know what came over him, but right out of the blue he came over to the house, told me everything about it and drew the map.

So here I was on this little dirt road, pulling my 12-foot john boat, when the road forked and Dave's map didn't. I did what everyone else does when confronted with this problem; first staring intently at one way then the other, with the same result everyone else gets. I still didn't know where to go.

After a minute or two the spirit of wisdom had yet to appear, so I flipped a mental coin and took the left fork. I soon had doubts about my decision, as the road got smaller and smaller and there was no place to turn around.

After five or six miles, at about five miles an hour, I was wishing I had stayed home. I was hot, tired and frustrated at having to keep my eyes on the road all the time so I could stay in the ruts, when suddenly I looked up and there was a town!

Just to keep the record straight it wasn't much of a town – – just an old Sinclair filling station, which was long out of business, a railroad depot but no tracks, and a general store with a piece of cotton hairpinned on the screen to keep the flies off. As far as I could tell there was only one living soul there, an old redneck sitting on the depot platform on a Nehi Orange crate.

He hadn't shaved in about a week and the tobacco in his cheek gave him the appearance of a contented milk cow. He sat blissfully, surveying his domain.

Looks like the jumping-off place, I thought to myself.

The road seemed to just run out, and since I did know that the only thing worse than being lost was being stupid, I pulled up to the platform, leaned out the window and asked the white lightnin' character what the name of the town was.

"This here's the Jumping Off Place," he said through yellow teeth.

21

There are some people we all expect to be wise guys; New York cab drivers, IRS men, and people you happen to be asking a favor from, but ain't no hick in the world gonna sit on a orange crate and cut me down for the fun of it, particularly in the mood I was in then.

"That did it!" I said in a loud voice, and made a great show of jumping out of the truck, slamming the door and stomping around in the dust while I rolled up my sleeves.

"Come on down offen that Nehi crate!"

Slowly he raised a tobacco stained finger and pointed to the sign on the depot. "That's what the sign says. Been sayin' it ever since I been here," he drawled.

It was rusty, but sure enough, I could make it out – – "Jumping Off Place."

To tell the truth I was still mad but kinda glad I didn't have to fight. You never know when a fellow is a biter. "Then maybe you can tell me where this road goes," I asked.

"I ain't never seen it go nowhare. Long as I been here it's been right thar." That guy was really asking for it. What a smart-ass.

"Jumping Off Place is a real dumb name for a town," I told him, trying to find some way to cut him down to size.

"Yep, I guess it is," he said. "'Cept it ain't really a town. It's a mighty useful place, though."

"If it ain't a town, then what is it?"

"This is where people come who realize they have made a mess out of their lives and jump off the edge of the earth." He never changed his expression.

That did it! I kicked that crate about twenty feet and grabbed him before his hind end hit the splinters.

"Hold on!" he said. "Look around you. There ain't no road leading outta here. The road you came in on is one-way. Don't that strike you strange? Look at that line of trees. See anything unusual? That's the edge of the earth."

I looked down his bony finger to the line of trees. Tall and slender, gently waving in the breeze. But all I could see on the other side of them was space!

A revelation slowly seeped through my mind. Something was bad wrong!

I turned him loose and stepped back, but even though the Nehi crate was gone, he never changed positions. He just continued sitting there like the crate was under him, chewing his cud.

"Uh huh. You ain't as dumb as you look," he said as he looked me in the eye. "You is seeing the light."

I was getting a little scared, but I was a lot more curious. "What do you mean, the ones who have made a mess of their lives come here to jump off the edge of the earth? You don't look like you have done so much with your life, and you ain't jumped."

"Well, I wouldn't say that now," he was giving me a glinty-eyed stare. "I been sittin' right here doing exactly this for over a thousand years, right here by the edge, givin' directions. And as long as I'm doing what I want to do, I'll never have to take the big leap."

He went on to explain that the Jumping-Off Place was for those who had always intended to do something different with their lives, but for some reason or other had never got around to doing it.

"They don't come until they get somewhere between forty and sixty-five years old, that's when they finally realize that they ain't *never* going to do whatever it is that they been wanting to do all their lives, and it's too much of a shock. That's when they just don't feel like resistin' any more, they give up, and fate sends them here."

"You oughta see 'em. The younger ones, why, they take a runnin' jump out into the big misty, while some of the old codgers just sort of toddle off the edge.

"Had a housewife down here last week. Always wanted to be some sort of interior decorator. She put it off until it was too late. Then she came down here and jumped. Did a swan dive. Day before that I had a doctor who always wanted to be a forester. Said to himself he was going to doctor until he had enough money to quit and take to the woods. He realized on his sixty-third birthday he wasn't never going to do it. Drove his Buick doctor's car right off the edge. Boy, that was something to see!" He laughed a downright disgusting laugh.

Finally he regained control of himself and continued.

"Those would-be book writers. Get a lot of them. Seems they always think way back in the back of their minds they are going to write a book and get rich and famous. That's sort of a crutch they lean on. When they finally realize they ain't gonna do it, they can't face life without the crutch, so they come here to me.

"'Course, I get all kinds. School teachers who intend to go back to school and get their masters, carpenters who plan to be contractors, rich business men who would like to get out of the rat race and tie salmon flies, the list goes on and on.

"They all have one thing in common," he said. "They keep putting it off and finding excuses and saying 'before long I'm gonna....but they never do, and then it's too late."

"What happens to them when they jump off?" I asked.

"They turn into shooting stars, boy. Gives 'em a second or two of glory, then it's all over. Didn't you ever wonder where shooting stars come from?"

We sat in silence for a minute, then he looked me straight in the face. "O. K., now it's your turn. Sure would appreciate it if you would try to do something spectacular – – maybe you could climb one of those trees and jump off. Ain't nobody done that in a year or so."

"You talk like somebody with a paper rear end," I told him. "I ain't jumpin' into the big misty now, next week or next year! There are a lot of things I intend to do, and I ain't give up yet! I must have come here by mistake!"

His eyes grew cold. "Ain't no mistake, boy. Fate don't send you here but for one reason. Now get on with it!"

I began grasping at straws. "You got it all wrong. The Jumping Off Place doesn't necessarily mean the ending place – – it could mean the beginning!"

He looked a little confused and I pressed harder – – "When folks are discouraged and come here, you could give them some words of encouragement and convince them it's not too late and send them back! You know as well as I do it ain't never too late. You been sittin' here a thousand years doing the wrong thing!"

He looked like he was about to cry, and I knew my argument had hit home.

24

"Instead of doing something terrible, you could do something positive for mankind, something that would make you proud of yourself. You don't seem too proud now."

Suddenly he raised his head. "You are right. I've been thinking I misunderstood what my mission here was. I'm full of magic, I know what to say to them to give 'em renewed hope. I can do It!"

We shook hands, and I was right proud of myself as I drove away on the narrow road. Suddenly, I was confronted by a hayseed riding a mule toward the Jumping Off Place.

"Please move out of my way," he said, "I got to get to that town up there. Something is pulling me."

"Hold on a minute, buddy. Why do you look so despondent?" As if I didn't know.

"I been diggin' taters all my life, but I always had hopes of running for office and being a politician. Today somebody asked me if I was elected to Congress what was the first thing I would do. I told them I would go on one of those junkets to Paris. I clean forgot the first duty of a politician is to raise taxes. It's all over for me, I ain't single-minded enough. I realize that now."

I asked him his name.

"Caleb Auntsy."

"Caleb, you go on down there to that town," I told him, "you are going to make a fine politician."

I let him by and drove on outa there proud as a fella could be.

Never did get to Dave's bass hole, but I kept his map in case I ever found my dreams running out of gas.

25

the I.R.S. Solution

*The kinder, gentler IRS will help you through
your little difficulties, just give them a chance. The
worst thing about most problems is they must
be faced, but once we do, most of the time
they are not as bad as they seem.*

I had a misunderstanding with the I.R.S. The whole thing
was pretty simple, I hadn't paid them what they said I
should have. I didn't dispute their figure; I thought it was
right, but that's where the whole thing changed from a misunderstanding to a problem. The problem was I didn't have any
money.

I went over to meet with them, and a very nice lady told me
my problem wasn't unique, there seemed to be a lot of people
who owed them money and none of them seemed to have any.

She went on to explain that I was now talking to a kinder,
gentler, I.R.S., and that instead of taking peoples homes, cars
and businesses they preferred to work it out some other way to
prevent hardship.

That seemed like a very good idea to me, and I told her so.
I also told her that her office was very nice, and that I thought
the finest people in the federal government worked for the
I.R.S. I also told her I believed in always being nice to people

26

no matter who they work for.

She thanked me for being a courteous customer, told me a person from a special division would be contacting me and I left her very nice office.

Now just so you have the proper perspective on this, I must tell you that I didn't owe them just a piddling little sum, but thousands of dollars. It wasn't because I was making so much money that I owed them, it was because I was president of a company that hadn't paid them, and I was liable for it personally. Ain't that a crock!

Anyway, now that I had met with them, I felt much better about it. Evidently they understood the problem and were willing to do the sensible thing.

It's sort of like living in a small village and knowing that there is a bear in the woods. No one has ever seen this bear, but everyone knows he is there. Now he might be a little bitty bear, but more than likely he is a great, giant grizzly bear that will soon come out and kill everyone. The more we worry about it the bigger this bear grows, and before long he is a King Kong bear, and we

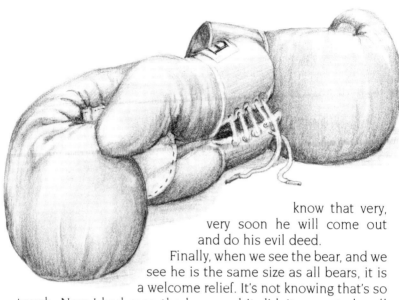

know that very,
very soon he will come out
and do his evil deed.

Finally, when we see the bear, and we
see he is the same size as all bears, it is
a welcome relief. It's not knowing that's so
tough. Now I had seen the bear, and it didn't seem to be all
that bad. A guy would contact me. Fair enough.

A few weeks went by. I didn't hear anything. I briefly considered giving them a call to perk 'em up a little, but discarded
that idea as plum *stupid*. The very next day the call came. A very
nice gentleman on the other end told me his name was James
Cholera from Remedies and Solutions, a new branch of the I.R.S.

"I would be delighted if you could see your way clear to
come to my office next Thursday at two o'clock," he said sweetly.
"I think I have figured out a solution to our mutual problem." I
told him how delighted I was to hear that, and if it didn't
involve me writing any checks I was sure I could handle it.

I was prompt and so was he. His office was nice too.
Government desk, government plants, and unsexy government
secretary. "I'll come right to the point, Mr. C, " he said, "you owe
us a lot of money. Fortunately, I have figured out a way for you
to pay it.

"Three months from today, at Caesars Palace in Las Vegas,
you will fight George Foreman in a boxing match. We have sold
the television rights for enough to pay your debt, and we
should make enough on the gate to be able to send a little to
the old agents' retirement home." He sat back, obviously
pleased with himself.

Say what?

I was in shock. It was several minutes before I could speak. Finally, I explained that I was no longer a young pup, that I had never even had on a pair of boxing gloves, and that it wouldn't be a boxing match, it would be a killing. And I would be the killee.

"Had you proposed this when I was 25 or so, I might have at least made a showing, but now – –"

"You didn't owe the money then," he said with the smugness of a man who knows he's right. " Look, I know it won't be easy, I understand how you feel. But it's the only way, and by golly, you are going to do it or else!"

So I had to do it. There was no getting around it. Please understand, it wasn't the fear of being hurt that I dreaded, it was the cotton-pickin' embarrassment! I was going to have to walk out in that ring, belly and all, and get slapped around for fun for awhile, then get knocked back to about 1958!

Everyone that I cared about would be there, plus millions more on t.v. I had no doubt it would get a good audience – – "Tune in tonight and watch a bozo get launched!" Or, "Make a pool with your friends on how long this zipper-head can go," or "If the bum lasts a minute you get half-off a fish sandwich at Hardees!"

Humiliation. Disgrace. From that moment on, I would always be known as "old fist in the face."

However, I am proud to report to you that once my fate was sealed, and that I did for sure understand that I couldn't get out of it, I started doing everything I could to get ready. By golly, they might laugh, I told myself, but I'm going to put a whipping on that dude!

I started getting into shape. Roadwork. Situps. After all, I had three months to get ready. I could whip anyone who ever lived if I had three months to get ready, I told myself. Light bag. Heavy bag. Hired a wino to be my sparring partner. Got bit twice and had to take shots.

I worked hard, real hard. But a tiny little voice kept telling me, no matter how hard I tried to convince myself otherwise, that I was going to get killed. I would just work harder. After several weeks of that I started getting a little muscle tone. I felt great. I would dance around, shadow box, bob and weave. I was getting ready, and I knew it. I heard about an ex-fighter who was shoveling donkey crap over at the zoo. I invited him over to watch my workout but all he wanted to do was sit there and laugh, so I made him leave.

Finally, the time came. I flew out a few days ahead so I could meet with the press. I had a press conference but no one showed up except a guy who wanted to sell me life insurance. That didn't do much for my confidence.

The night of the fight, sitting in my dressing room, I could hear the large, ravenous crowd screaming with frenzy. I tried to work up some confidence, but could not. It was no use. I was going to be absolutely humiliated. Right in front of God and the world. Even my mama was going to laugh. My children would find out I wasn't Superman like I told them I was. In a few more moments, it would be crunch time.

The crowd was screaming and shoving as I walked down the aisle to the ring. I was so terrified I wouldn't look up, but kept a steady gaze on the top of my shoes. I climbed in the ring and looked up at the ceiling.

Suddenly, a mighty roar. George Foreman was coming into the ring.

I kept staring at the ceiling as I took off my robe, and the ring announcer's voice seemed far away as he introduced the fighters. Polite applause for me, great roar for George.

All right, quit being such a big baby, I told myself. I was getting mad. Not at the world for being so unfair, but at myself. "Pull yourself together and go out there and do the best you possibly can," I told myself, "you can do anything, remember? Quit being such a big sissy!"

It was time to prove what I was made out of, and suddenly, like an old Viking, I was ready to go down fighting. I whirled around and there stood George, muscles bulging, fire in his eye, except – – he was a little bitty guy, his head only came up to my knee!

The bell rang, and he rushed toward me. "George," I yelled, what is the matter with you?"

"I've been sick, you turkey!" And he started raining little blows on my shin. I've always been able to take a punch to my shin, especially by a little fist wearing a itsy-bitsy boxing glove. I danced around and made him chase my shins, even did an Ali shuffle and made him miss a time or two. Finally I hit him on top of the head and cold-cocked the little sucker. I ran around the ring with arms raised while they revived George. At that moment in time, I loved everybody. Even I.R.S. agents.

George was a real gentleman. Later he came to my dressing room and I told him how much I had dreaded having to fight him.

"Let that be a positive experience for you," he said, "problems are seldom as big as they seem once you face them."

(From a dream I had the night before I was scheduled to meet with the I.R.S.)

the Retriever from Hell

The good thing about dogs is you can have them custom made. Eventually you can get exactly what you want, but you better think it through carefully. Sue and Lucky made a great team.

I hate Golden Retrievers. Hate 'em, hate 'em, hate 'em. They are big sneaky bullies. They will bite you. That is, they will bite you if you are a child, a small woman or if you have been sick. If you are a big tough dude they won't come within grabbing distance. They just pick on critters smaller and weaker than they are, unless there is more than one, then they may gang up on a lab or something.

Our family had a black lab for sixteen years. Old Ash. Ash was a good old dog, a good retriever and an outstanding family member. But the best thing about Ash was he hated Goldens almost as much as I did.

Friend of mine down the street got a pair of Golden puppies. Both males. When they grew up, you hardly ever saw one without the other. They were inseparable. The reason they were inseparable was Ash. If he ever caught one of them alone he would beat him to a bloody pulp. In fact, in his younger days

Lucky Boykin

he could handle both of them at one time. And there was nothing he had rather do. When he was dying, and laying on the ground and couldn't get up, I went to look for the two Goldens. I knew if I could find either of them Ash would have come up from there. Might have given him a few more days.

I never knew why Ash hated Goldens so bad, but I sure know why I do. It was because of Lucky. Lucky was my Boykin Spaniel. Lucky wasn't just a Boykin, he was a world champion Boykin. In case you don't know about Boykins, they are about the size of a cocker spaniel but a little leggier. For some types of retrieving, they are unbeatable. A dove field in September in the South, for instance. They can take the heat.

I could kill a limit of doves and never get off my seat. Lucky would get every one, then when the shoot was over find lost birds for everyone else. Lucky was special to me, he rode in the front of the truck. Boykins think they are human, and expect to be treated that way.

But Lucky had a problem. Golden Retrievers. When you go to a dove shoot, the first thing one does is flock up. Shake hands with the men, kiss the ladies, admire the dogs and check out new guns or whatever. Purely social. This was the bad time for Lucky. About a third of the retrievers one finds in the field are Labs, about a third are Goldens, and the rest in our area are Boykins. The labs would generally stay in their trucks, or sit by their masters during the conversation, but the Goldens would all come looking for Lucky and take turns whipping his butt.

Would a Golden mess with a lab? Never. Would a Golden mess with a Boykin if their sizes were similar? Never. But a Boykin is a little guy, and that made him bait for the cowardly Goldens.

Lucky was brave, and would never back down. But he was just no match for the big Goldens.

Me and Lucky both were getting fed up. It got to where the Goldens recognized my truck, and when they saw us coming they would all start salivating. They couldn't wait to grab poor Lucky. I was determined to do something about it.

One night I ran across a quote from Theodore Roosevelt, where he said an Airedale could do anything any other dog could, and when it was over whip the other dog. That sounded interesting, but I sort of forgot about it.

A few weeks later I ran across a piece about a champion pit bull in England. The piece said this champion dog was matched in a dog fight with a big Airedale a farmer owned. It was a fierce fight, the piece reported, and after 55 minutes the pit bull was winning. It went on to say that the Airedale was a silent fighter, and up until then had made no sound whatever. The article said the pit bull won for the first 55 minutes, but 60 minutes into the fight the pit bull was dead. The Airedale never made a sound.

The next month I went out to New Mexico on an elk hunt. In casual conversation with my guide, he told me he hunted bears and lions in the off season. Turned out he had his own pack of hounds which he was very proud of, and he took me to look them over. He had eight or ten fine hounds all right, but also in the pen were two old scroungy looking warriors that sort of stood off to themselves.

"Those are my hunting Airedales," he said proudly. "If a bear comes down out of a tree they make him pay!"

I asked him how such fierce dogs were around the hounds. He said they never started fights, and were extremely easy to get along with. "Every once in a while one of these big hounds will decide to jump on one of them, and it's not long before he realizes he's made a terrible mistake."

A delightful thought was growing in my feeble little mind. It would take some time, but I was going to fix those back-stabbing cowardly Goldens!

"Where can I get the meanest, fiercest Airedale? I mean, I want one that could whip a grizzly bear," I asked.

He fished in his wallet and produced a telephone number. "This man's name is R.C. Wallace. He has a strain of upgraded Airedales. He sells puppies, but I have to warn you, they are dogs from hell!" It was music to my ears.

When I called R.C., he said he didn't have any males for sale, but had a bitch puppy that was out of the two "best lion dogs that ever lived." My dogs love to die, he said. I bought the puppy.

That was a great little dog. I named her Amanda. I put her

in a pen out back and waited for her to grow up. And did she ever! When she came into heat, I took her over and put her in the pen with Lucky. "Just be real careful, little guy, and don't start any fights," I told him. Lucky always thought he was the greatest lover alive, and that Spring he proved it. Amanda produced three puppies.

They were also fine! They had inherited Lucky's strong retrieving instinct, and the size and fighting spirit of Amanda. But I wasn't through. While on a visit to South Georgia I heard about a man who had crossed a pit bull with an alligator. "No way," I told the friend who had told me about it. "One is a mammal, the other a Republican. It will never take."

"Maybe not," he said, "but he claims he did. He's a crazy old coot so who knows."

I looked him up. Yes, he said, he did have a dog for sale. Two generations removed from the alligator.

"Is he trained? I asked.

"Sho."

I drove out to see the dog and I noticed when he was bringing him out the first ten feet of the rope he was tied to ran through a pipe so he could hold him off.

"Thought you said he was trained."

"I did."

"What's he trained to do?"

"Bite yore arm off."

He was my kind of dog.

I took him home, and later bred him to one of Lucky and Amanda's offspring, Big Crunch. Big Crunch only had one puppy, but the first time I saw him I knew my prayers had been answered. I was tempted to name him Wino, but I didn't want half the guys on the field coming when I called him, so I named him Sue, like Johnny Cash.

I knew I really had something when Sue was six weeks old. He bit a plug out of a chain-link fence. I put Sue through a year-and-a-half training program, every day showing him a picture of a Golden Retriever, then giving him a piece of raw meat. Eventually, he got the picture.

Let me describe this wonderful dog to you. Standing flat-footed, his back was about up to a man's waist. He had a great, massive chest, and a head that looked like a beer barrel. He had a long snout, sort of scaley-looking lips, and a fine set of teeth all the way down, sort of like a Mako shark. He was chocolate brown like Lucky, and had green eyes like some sort of prehistoric monster. The things I just told you about were the pretty part of old Sue. The ugly part was his disposition.

Finally Sue's training was complete, and just in time too, because dove season was opening the next Saturday. I sure was glad. I had 200-pounds of new retriever ready to go!

On the day of the first shoot, I slid the seat back as far as it would go in my pickup and put Sue in the floor. Lucky took his customary seat next to the window so he could hang his arm out.

The gathering place was an old farmhouse, complete with big oaks in the yard and plenty of shade. When we drove up, I saw that everyone was there, and it was business as usual. The hunters were standing in little groups, talking, and the labs were behaving themselves in their places. There were seven or eight Goldens, though, cruising the place, including King, Lucky's main nemesis.

We drove up and stopped, and King saw us. He remembered the truck from the year before, and shivered with delight. He came on the run. Around the truck he went to Lucky's side, and I opened the door.

Everything had worked out just fine for big stud King up to that point, but it wasn't Lucky that jumped out – – it was the retriever from Hell!

I couldn't see what was happening, but Lucky was laughing his fool head off.

King disappeared from view, and as I was frantically racing around the truck I heard a brief scuffle, maybe, two seconds, and that was it. Sue was sitting on the ground with this big contented smile on his face, Lucky, still in the truck, was laughing so hard I thought he was having a convulsion, and King was nowhere to be seen.

Then Sue gave this big burp – – and two or three beautiful golden hairs came floating along on the breeze. Sue had eaten

King!

The other Goldens got a look at Sue and took off, and every time, Lucky would lay down on the ground and laugh like a fool.

Of course, King was never found. Lucky was killed a year later by a pickup while he was chasing a sexy little French poodle. I still have Amanda and her puppies. Sue was too much to handle, so I sent him to South Georgia. Got a report awhile back. Seems there wasn't a single Golden in a five-county area down there.

C.A.T.S.

You can tear around the lake beating the water to a froth if you want to, and you can get money on your mind and work yourself to death if you like, but you will never be a member of this organization!

It was still dark. (That's a good way to signify morning. Just like "getting dark" most certainly means late afternoon.) When I drove up to the diner where I was supposed to meet Clancy I could see him inside at the counter, drinking coffee. It was a little cool early in the morning like this, even though it was late May. The diner was all yellow inside, with drops of condensation running down the windows.

"Bout time," he said, even though I was ten minutes early. I mounted a stool and ordered coffee.

"Been having some trouble with my motor, " he said like it was an official announcement. "But I got it out of the shop yestiddy. It's gonna run good today, and we are gonna kill some hawgs."

Clancy was good for knowin' all the hip talk. It was too early to be very sharp, but I did notice that his green jump suit

with B.A.S.S. on the sleeve clashed with the yellow of the diner.

We were both anxious to get going, so we drained our cups and walked outside, where the yellow light cast an unreal glow on his rig, a 15-foot fiberglass bass boat and 140-hoss Merc, complete. And I mean complete. Carpet on the floor, racks for holding rods, electric anchor putter outer and taker inner, electric motor, depth finder, steering wheel with star dust, built-in ice chests, captain's chairs mounted on little masts so we could get above 'em, the whole works.

A $20,000 rig pulled by a $600 Chevy, piloted by a man in a green jumpsuit with a one-track mind. That's having your priorities in order.

After a short run to the lake, we launched the boat and I hardly had time to settle in before the race began. We tore off up the lake, ran about a minute, and Clancy slowed down to about the speed of sound and began staring at his depth finder. "Here it is," he yelled over the roar of the motor as he cut the switch, mashed a button to let the anchor down and make his first cast, all in one motion. By the time I had rigged up to make a cast, Clancy had cast about twenty times, caught two small bass and was letting the anchor up. "Ain't nothin' here," he yelled. Varoom! The motor started and we were off again. "If they're here, they will hit the worm. If they don't hit the worm, they ain't here." I think that's what he said. I was hanging on for dear life.

We repeated the performance all over that poor lake, literally whipping the water to a froth, but with slim result. "I don't understand it," he said, lying down on the bottom of the boat. He was worn out from all that casting and operating his B.A.S.S. approved equipment.

By lunchtime we had five small bass, one worn out arm and one rapidly growing ulcer. After that mad dashing about, I was convinced I would never be able to lay down and go to sleep again – – ever.

Since the bass in the lake didn't seem to care very much about us, even if all our equipment was officially approved, we decided to take out and try the river, maybe the stripers were tearing it up. It wasn't much trouble though – – Clancy had an approved trailer and an approved winch, and soon we were tooling down the highway.

After we launched the boat in approved fashion, we ran up the river about five miles when suddenly the motor coughed, sputtered and died. We coasted to a stop. "Your motor stopped," I announced. "Betcha that guy didn't fix it."

Clancy sat there a second or two, staring off into space, then jumped up and fished his checklist out of the drywell. There was a tiny patch on the upper right hand corner of his clipboard – B.A.S.S. Clancy ran his finger down the list. "Nope," he said, "all checked."

"Maybe we're out of gas," I ventured, not knowing if common sense has anything to do with modern fishing. "Cain't be," he held out the clipboard to me, "see, it's checked."

The gas tank was in its proper place to my left, and I leaned over, unscrewed the cap and looked in. Nothing but airy blackness. "Either your checklist is lying or this gas tank is," I said, "it's empty."

We were stranded five miles up the river. There was no sign of life in any direction.

I could see Clancy was awfully upset, so as to make things as bad for him as I possibly could I began to sing some of my most requested numbers. It didn't help him any, I'll tell you that. Made me feel good though.

Presently another fisherman came around the bend. Well, you couldn't really call him a fisherman – – he had neither motor, depth finder or catbird seat. He was paddling an old cypress bateau that had three inches of freeboard on each side and he had to be the slowest moving fellow I had ever seen.

"We've got trouble," Clancy yelled. "Can you help?"

"Shore," the man said, and paddled toward us. As he drew near I could tell he was my kind of guy. He was wearing an old straw hat, air conditioned by two holes in one side, a pair of bib overalls, and a beat-up old pair of brogans. He sported neither shirt nor socks.

As he drew alongside, I noticed a patch on the hat, another on the strap of his overalls, and a third on the heel of his brogans. The all featured the same four letters: C. A. T. S.!

I watched for a minute, then had to ask. "What do those patches stand for?"

"Why, this is the official patch of the Catfishing Association and Temperance Society. I'm a charter member."

That seemed a little funny to me, but the guy seemed to be real relaxed and at peace with the world. "What do you fellows do?" I asked, hoping I didn't sound unusually stupid.

"We go after the big calves that swim deep." That was a straight enough answer.

"Well, what about the temperance part in your name. I don't guess you fellows drink."

"Shecks, we'll drink just about anything. I took drunk myself this past weekend. Sunday came and went and I didn't even know it." He gave us a big grin. "The temperance in our name means self-constraint in action. We exhibit self-control while fishing."

There was a rusty old can of worms on the seat, and you guessed it, it proudly wore the patch, C.A.T.S. So did his old cane pole, his boat, and a can of sardines and soda crackers he had half finished. C.A.T.S. approved lunch, it said.

My next question was a model of decorum and intelligence. "Catchin' any?"

"Got five or six squealers and one small calf about twenty pounds." He reached for a venetian cord stringer. Sure enough, C.A.T.S. approved. "I missed a big calf this mornin' though. Had her on for a minute, but my hook straightened."

His paddle was of tupelo and constant use had almost obliterated the C.A.T.S. stamp, but it was still in good shape. His Tampa Nugget tackle box looked the worse for wear, though.

Upon further questioning, he told of winning the big C.A.T.S. catfishing tournament earlier in the year. "It was a tough field," he said modestly. "Those fellows could paddle slow, I'm telling you. Five hours after the start wasn't a single contestant more'n twenty yards from the starting line, and most of them had caught a pot full and hadn't even changed worms! The prizes were great, too. I won first, so I didn't have to take nothin', second man had to take a new tackle box, third place man had to go to Atlanta and watch a ball game, and the pore feller who won the booby prize had to take an all expense paid trip to Paris for two weeks – – nearly killed him."

This club was sounding better by the minute. "How much does it cost to be a member of C.A.T.S.?" I asked.

"Cost?" He shook his head. "Don't cost nothin'. If you are a member, they send *you* a check every year for ten dollars. We ain't got no dues, we don't elect any officers, we don't give any awards to each other, and we don't have any newsletter we have to read neither."

"Gosh, that sounds great! What are the qualifications for membership?"

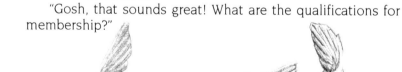

"Well, if you think fishin' is a contest, we ain't got no use for you." He looked over at Clancy. "But if you are serious about membership, you got to get two sorry, good-for-nothing fellows in your town that know you to swear that you know how to take life for what it is. They got to say that you don't get uptight if you ain't making a lot of money or if you have to drive an old car. They got to swear that sometime you just sit in the swing or out in the yard in a chair or maybe you lay down in the grass and let the world roll on. And they got to say they know you can enjoy where you are and what you are doing, and you ain't never wished you were somewhere else!"

He paused for effect. "And it would help if you took drunk every once in a while and barf in the yard!"

I told him I thought I could qualify. "I'm the sorriest, slowest fellow I know. I'll take a break from taking a break. I'll leave work early to make up for coming in late."

"Maybe so, but you sure keep bad company." He looked at Clancy again. "What you fellows want me to do for you?"

"We're out of worms," I said. "Can you loan us a few? We wanted to drift down to the landin', seems the current is slow enough."

He gave us the worms, and a brick to drag behind if we moved too fast. I caught a few squealers and a small calf on the way back, but Clancy didn't even fish. He was busy reading his B.A.S.S. – – approved "In Case of Emergency" book.

Skippy Jackson

I've been told that one foot under the surface
of the ground it stays 78 degrees all the time.
Ants know about that kind of stuff. They are
smart. They also like to party down, and
boy, do they have some great music!

Y ou know how it is when you sit on a deer stand. When you first get off the truck there is so much to see you don't notice much, but the longer you sit, the more you notice the little things, the things that really count.

This little adventure started out that way, a deer stand in the low country of South Carolina, an hour past the time I should have been picked up. Earlier I had noticed an old bottle half-buried in the dirt, but I hadn't been bored enough to investigate. Finally, with nothing better to do, I walked over and gave it a kick with my Russell Bird Shooters. The bottle jumped free, and I picked it up.

It was an interesting old bottle, no marking of any kind, but being a man of the world I could tell it had been hand-blown, somewhere around 1840, I guessed. The more I looked at the little bottle, the more interested I became, finally reaching the point of taking it over to the ditch and washing it out.

It was about half-full of dirt, which washed out easily enough. But to my surprise, once the dirt was gone, there remained a single, gleaming little white pill, about the size of a pea but seemingly with a hard coating. I wiped it off on my britches leg and put it on a nearby stump, and there it sat, gleaming white.

After a bit I began to lose interest in the bottle and gain interest in the little white pill. However, there ain't much a fellow can do with a little white pill. I picked it up and looked at it two or three times, then put it back. And there it sat.

I don't know if you have them or not, but for most of my life there have been two little guys in my head that always take opposite sides on every issue. The one who gets me in the most trouble is called Lester. Lester is also the one who has brought me the most pleasure. The other guy is Buddy. Buddy is always against taking chances. He has saved my life many times.

The way it works is like this. I'll see an attractive lady, and I'll send the thought out that I might pinch her. Lester responds immediately, urging me on. "It's crowded in this elevator, ain't no way would she ever know who did it," he'll say. "Her rear ain't more'n two inches from your hand, do it!" Buddy, of course, will not stand for it. "What kind of person are you? Don't you know to do a common thing like that would distress that young lady? Besides, she <u>will</u> know, and she'll slap the crap out of you!"

Buddy's arguments usually win out, because they make the most sense, but if one lived by Buddy's rules a fellow would have many, many dull days in his life. I appreciate having both of them, because I

could never make up my mind by myself.

That day it wasn't long before Lester and Buddy started up about that dang pill.

"Swallow that pill," Lester said.

"Are you crazy?" said Buddy. "We don't know nothin' bout that pill. It might be poison. Some Yankee might have dropped it."

"Nothing ventured, nothing gained," Lester argued. "You ain't a pure-tee Southern gentleman iffen' you don't swallow that little pill. It ain't bigger'n nothin. It would slide right down!"

It wasn't a good day for me. I was tired of all the conflict. I snatched the little pill up and swallowed it. Lester was right, it slid right down.

At first, nothing happened; then this strange feeling of well-being began to come over me. "Must have been some sort of tranquilizer," I thought. Then I noticed something really weird begin to happen. I was slowly but surely getting smaller and smaller! I guess I should have been terrified, but I had this great calm feeling at the time, and I really didn't get too excited about it.

Smaller and smaller I shrank. The log on which I was previously sitting was now head high, and still I was getting smaller. A few more seconds and the grass, formerly at my feet, was up to my chest, and on down I went. Finally, at about an eighth of an inch tall, I stopped shrinking.

"That was one helluva diet pill," Lester said, but I was in no mood for him and I yelled at him to mind his own business and shut up!

The grass had turned into a formidable jungle and there were creatures, some smaller than me, some not, scurrying about. Believe me, it's another world down there in that grass.

I wandered about for awhile, my short legs clearly not made for the terrain, when suddenly I came face to face with a large ant who was sitting quietly, giving me the fisheye.

"Boo!" I yelled, but it didn't frighten him a bit.

I jumped at him and stomped my feet and made all kinds of threatening gestures but he just watched in amazement. You can't believe my surprise when he spoke!

"What'sa matter with you boy? You don't feel so good?"

That was all I needed. An Italian ant. "Slap him," Lester said. But I had learned my lesson about listening to him by now.

"What are you doing talking?" I asked, "Ants can't talk, least, I didn't know they could," I said as I looked for an avenue of escape.

"Aw, we can do a lot of things that *people* don't know we can do," he said with a southern accent.

"What kind of ant are you?"

"I'm a fire ant. Go by the name of Skippy Jackson," he said. "How did you get so tiny? I ain't never seen a human as small as you."

"I took a little white pill I found. I'm hoping it will soon wear off and I'll get back to regular." I felt a little silly talking to an ant. "A fire ant, huh? You guys have a bad reputation in the regular world."

"Well, we ain't as bad as you think," he said. "I know we get a little carried away when our home is being destroyed, and some of you folks get stung, but we could all live together if yau'll would show some common sense."

We talked some more, and for an ant, he really wasn't a bad guy. I got to liking him pretty good, and he invited me home with him to meet some of his friends. He seemed to think my reduced size could be a great opportunity for increased communication between ant and man.

49

I didn't see what I could lose, so I climbed on his back and away we went. Boy, he could really run. With all those legs it didn't matter what we had to go over, there was always two or three legs on the ground steady runnin'. I know it couldn't have been more than fifty or sixty feet, but it was miles at my tiny size to the fire ant hill. He covered it in nothing flat.

As we neared the hill, I began to notice other fire ants, all carrying something, alone or in teams, some carrying things many times larger than their own bodies. We ran right up the side of the hill and through an opening. I immediately became aware of how cool it was inside, even though the sun was bearing down.

Everywhere there was furious activity. Lifting, moving, cutting, building, running to and fro.

"We work awful hard," Skippy said. "Everybody in a fire ant hill has to work, but unlike you humans, you never hear any griping about it."

In every room there was a fascinating display of teamwork and discipline. I asked Skippy what they ate. "We are meat eaters, primarily boll weevil larvae and grasshoppers, but a lot of insects are good stuff," he said.

"I've never seen anyone work so hard," I remarked, and it was true.

"Well, it ain't all work. We do work hard during the day, but have you ever wondered what goes on in an ant hill when the sun goes down? Boy, do we party down! There's a stage show every night, the greatest music you ever heard and a different kind of dance for every night in the week. We party until about three, hit the sack for a couple of hours and are ready to go again at daylight." He seemed proud of the whole thing.

I asked if they ever ran out of food, and he said they stored up in the summer for the winter, stockpiling grasshoppers and boll weevils in holes under the mound.

"There was one time though, when we had more food than we knew what to do with – – a real time of plenty. It was when your agriculture department tried to poison us by dropping stuff out of airplanes. Seems like they managed to poison almost everything around but us." He seemed a bit sad. "They killed birds by the jillion, especially quail. In fact, they killed just about everything around that had been killing us."

"That might be so, " I told him, "but there are times when people don't want you guys around, like in yards and pastures and such."

"We know about that, in fact, you fellows do all kinds of things to get rid of us. Most of them don't work " He started to laugh. "Awhile back little Ridie Goforth came running in to tell us of a fellow who was pouring gasoline on a neighboring hill and setting it on fire. We knew we would be next, so we immediately ran down to our storerooms and brought all our grasshoppers and boll weevils up to the top of the mound where the guy barbecued them medium rare. After everything cooled off, we took them back to the storeroom, and our kitchen crews took six months off, their cooking done."

"Well, what do you recommend we do to let you know we don't want you around? We can't just let you have the run of the place," I asked.

He said there were several types of poisons around that worked, did not harm other wildlife, and were always effective if they were applied directly to each ant hill.

Suddenly I began growing!

"Quick," I shouted, "let's get outside!"

We ran outside just in time. Another few seconds and I would have been bursting through the ceiling. I shook hands with Skippy. It was a tearful goodbye. "I'm afraid I won't be seeing you anymore," I said, "there was only one pill in the bottle."

I was several inches high by that time, and could barely hear him. "Try to get them to spray some more of that stuff out of airplanes," he shouted.

Soon I was back to normal size, and as I picked up my gun, I saw a pickup coming up the road.

"I sure am sorry," the driver apologized. "We forgot all about you over here. What have you been doing all this time?"

"I went down in that ant hill," I said, pointing to Skippy's lowrise.

He didn't say another word all the way back to the house.

the Last Regiment

*Things may not always be what they seem,
but you better be careful down in the swamp, there
may be things there you hadn't counted on.*

I think there is a time in every man's life when he wants a boat. The time I wanted one was from the time I was born until I was about forty.

It seemed every time I got a little money ahead something more important would come along and claim it, like buying groceries or getting one of the kids sewed up, so I just never could get enough together to get it done.

Finally, almost unbelievably, all the stars were in correct alignment and I was actually getting a good size tax refund. Best of all, my wife, kids, grocery store, graveyard lot payment folks, my lifetime membership to the spa with all day swimming on Sunday or Al's Garage didn't know anything about it.

I still wouldn't have a boat if it hadn't been for my friend Buster. He came up to me at the half time of a poetry reading — — "I found the perfect boat for you when you get the money," he announced, like he doubted I ever would — — "It's a fourteen foot

Boston Whaler with a forty horse. Guy I know wants to sell it."

He gave me the seller's name and address. And it still wouldn't have amounted to anything, but the next morning when I went to pick up my mail, the check I had been expecting for six weeks was sitting in that box like a golden egg in a goose's nest.

I learned long ago that you can't tempt fate. It was a sign, and by God, it was time for me to stand up and be counted! It was a time for action! I would have given the cry of the great bull ape had I not been in a house of the federal government, because you know how it is, once a dull mind has been made up – –.

Now that I had the hot little check in my hand, I drove over to the boat's house to negotiate a price, keeping in mind that I had not, mind you, rode in here on a load of watermelons and that I knew the value of things, especially boats and my money.

Knock on the door. Working man's house. I could see the boat in the carport, covered by a tarp. Two good signs – – in the carport, and tarp on the boat. Slightly fat lady comes to the door – – yes, her husband does have a boat for sale and if I will wait just a minute she will get him up. Works night shift.

Tall skinny guy. Pencil thin mustache. He says the boat is in real good shape, he's only had it for a year and he wants $4,000 cash or good check. I figure he's behind on his truck payment, his house payment, his boat payment or his alimony

payment. Any guy that has a pencil thin mustache has had more than one wife. I offer $2,000.

"I'll take $3900 cash, but that's as low as I'm gonna go," he said.

I looked at the boat. I thought of all those striped bass, some at the thirty-pound mark, flopping in the bottom, not to mention all the other good stuff, like putting it in and taking it out, and me being the supervisor of the whole operation. Boats do a lot of good things for a guy beside getting him across the water. Wind in hair kind of stuff.

"You got any life preservers?"

"There are four in the boat," he said. "They go with the deal."

I have always been a tough negotiator. I wrote the check.

By then it was almost mid-afternoon, and I was definitely in a hurry as I hooked up the boat behind my truck, filled the gas tanks and hurried down to the Wateree River for a test run.

The river was a little high, but I had no trouble getting the new boat, my new boat, launched and running downriver. I'm telling you the truth, it ran like a dream! I opened her up. I throttled her back. I cut left, I cut right. I went trolling speed. I weaved in and out of trees. I went flat out so fast I was a cotton pickin' blur. This boat, my boat, was everything I had ever hoped it would be. I was so happy, so satisfied! So proud of myself!

The motor quit.

I started checking. It's getting gas. Nothing has come loose. I tried to start it again. No luck. I fumed. I fussed. I did everything I knew to do, and I couldn't get it started.

All this time I was drifting with the current down the river. As I worked on the motor, I guess maybe thirty minutes – – I wasn't paying any attention where I was or where I was going, and when I looked up I was on a part of the river I had never seen before. It was getting late, in fact, the evening mist had begun to settle on and around the river, but I wasn't worried. Put out to be sure, but not worried. All I had to do was drift on down the river until I got to a bridge or road, paddle over to the side, beach the boat, walk out, and tomorrow get Buster to help me get the boat out and back to Boogie Bear's Marina for a quick fix.

I drifted. And drifted. Nothing.

I was starting to get just a little bit panicky, when in the distance, through the mist, I could make out what appeared to be an old road running down the swamp to the river. It wasn't much of a road, didn't look like it had been used since Caesar was a pup. But it was all I had, and I was taking it.

I paddled over to the side, and pulled the boat up good and secure. I didn't have anything with me I needed to take, so as soon as I was satisfied the boat would stay put I started walking up the path.

I'll bet you I hadn't gone thirty feet when I heard a sound that sent cold chills up my backbone! Out of the mist, and really close, somebody cocked the hammer of an old-fashioned muzzleloader, a metallic click so close, and so deadly, it literally froze me in my tracks!

"Don't move, Yankee." It was a voice ever bit as cold and deadly as the hammer click. Move? I wasn't about to move. I'm not ashamed to tell you I was scared stiff.

Several seconds passed, and although I could hear movement, I still hadn't seen anyone. Suddenly out of the mist the shapes of men appeared, slowly moving toward me with .58 caliber muzzleloaders trained on my heart.

" What's going on, fellers?" I had to say something. "Yau'll coon huntin?"

They didn't say anything. Just walked around me with a slow creaky movement, ready to blow me to bits.

I thought I was scared then, but that wasn't anything like I felt when I got a better look at them. First I noticed they were wearing uniforms, or rather, clothes that had been uniforms at one time. They were torn and ragged, and in evidence of much repair; sort of a grey in color, but most of the color had long gone. But the most astonishing thing – – they were old! I don't mean just barnyard old, I mean ancient! Old drawn faces, white whiskers, thin lips; in fact, all of them were thin as rails. But the thing that really got me were their eyes! Burning dark orbs that shone with an energy straight from hell! Forty pairs of eyes that literally seemed to burn my skin with their gaze, looking at me like a hungry redneck looking at a plate of fried chicken.

"Call the captain," a voice said. We waited. Soon, horses hooves coming down the road. The rider made a slow dismount, and creaked up to me. Now, I'm telling you this man was old! Same raggedy old uniform, same piercing hot eyes.

"What have you got here, boys?" He asked as he looked me up and down.

A man with sergeant's stripes spoke. "Caught us a Yankee disguised as an idiot. Was sneakin' down the road."

The old captain put his nose about an inch from mine.

"How many more Yankees are with you, boy?"

Now I can take a lot of things, but this was the second time since I had beached my boat that I had been called a Yankee, and enough was enough. "Listen, you old goat, I ain't a Yankee and there ain't nobody with me. I got lost on the river when my motor quit and all I want to do is walk out of here and go home. You old guys better quit pointing guns at folks and go on back to Magnolia Manor or wherever you're from!"

He wasn't convinced.

"You don't sound like a Yankee, and as ugly as you are you don't look like any Yankee I ever saw, but we have to be real careful," he said, backing off a little bit. He sent a man to check out the boat.

"It's there all right," the soldier reported, "a boat with some kind of machinery on the back. Might be some sort of steam turbine."

More questions. Who is my family? What county are they from and how long have they been there? What church do we belong to? Finally, I was able to convince them I was who I said

I was. I even showed them my drivers license, which had no effect at all, which seemed strange to me.

Little by little, they began to relax, and I got up courage enough to ask the important question – – "Who are you guys?

"We are Company D, Third Regiment, Georgia Volunteers! Captain Hugh Smiley at your service, sir!" I don't have to tell you he said it with a lot of pride.

"But why are you here in this swamp? " I have always been a slow learner, and at that point I didn't have a clue.

"We were ordered by Col. Culverhouse to hold the Charleston highway where it crossed the Wateree River, and by God, we've held it. And we'll continue to hold it until ordered otherwise."

"Captain, when were you given that order?" A tiny light was beginning to glow in my brain, but it couldn't be!

The old man reached inside his beautiful torn old grey coat and brought out a yellowing scrap of paper, and there in the colonel's own handwriting was the date, Sept. 11, 1861.

"It's incredible," I said, "how long have you been here?" I was trying to work the numbers in my head and was having a hard time with it.

A wistful look came over the Captain's face. "I don't know, we sort of lost track of time, and then we didn't hear anything for so long!" Suddenly he looked up.

"Tell me, son, give me the war news!" he grabbed me by the arm, and I knew that I was the first person he had seen in all that time. I also knew that these old men had been in that swamp for over 130 years, carrying out their orders. No one can live that long normally, there had to be something that kept them going, and I knew what it was. It was the Cause, and their complete dedication to that Cause. A willingness to give every-thing, to sacrifice beyond sacrifice, a feeling so strong that it had rescinded the laws of nature! I also knew that if they knew the war was over, and the cause was lost, they would be doomed. I could never tell them.

"Well, Lee and his brave boys won a great victory at Fredericksburg, couldn't save the town, but boy they cleaned up on the Yankees when they tried to move against the heights south of town, and it was the Georgia boys fighting out of an old sunken road that did it," I told them, desperately trying to remember some Civil War history.

"Then the war moved further west," I continued, and at a place in Virginia called Chancellorsville Stonewall Jackson rolled 'em up like a rug!"

"Hot damn!," the old captain slapped his knee, " I always knew that Stonewall was a comer! But tell me son, is Lee moving on Washington yet?"

"Lord, you folks have been in this swamp a long time," I said to forty real old faces.

"Longstreet took Washington years ago. Lincoln got away though, you know what a slippery rascal he has always been. Newark, New Jersey is the capital of the Yankees now. Could have taken that too, but when Longstreet's boys got a look at it they didn't want it. Thought they would let the Yankees keep it for punishment."

"But tell me," I said to a sergeant standing nearby, " how have you boys been making it down here in the swamp all these years? How do you get enough to eat?" He explained that some of the fellows began farming years ago, and there were wild hogs all over the swamp. Of course, he said there were deer and turkeys too, "and we've managed to make it o.k. and guard the road too."

"If this is the Charleston highway, didn't you ever wonder why no one ever came through here?" Seemed a logical question to me.

"We figured there wasn't anybody that wanted to go to Charleston," the Captain said. "You know how stuck up and uppity they are down there."

"That long," I thought, but let it drop.

Everyone was completely relaxed by now, evidently I had been judged and found trustworthy. But something was burning my skin, one of those eyes was still turned on me full blast. Looking around, I didn't see anyone looking at me. The men were rolling cigarettes, checking their guns and talking over the war news I had just given them, but someone had their eye on me and that was for sure.

Then I noticed the horse. That old bag of bones was standing off to the side, one leg crossed like he owned the woods, with a big black eye fixed on me like a searchlight. I went closer and looked in his eye. Looked just like any horse's eye from a distance, but when I got up close, that big kind pool of a horse's eye had a tiny fire burning way down deep, a tiny little flame that never flickered.

I called the Captain over. "Your horse is looking at me," I told him, "and I don't like it."

"Well, he's just suspicious by nature," the Captain told me, "don't worry about it, he's get over it soon."

"Captain, how long have you had this horse?"

"Why, I don't know. I rode in here on him, and I had him a few years before that."

I couldn't believe it. Commitment to the Cause could explain the long life of the men here, but the horse?

I looked in his eye again, and the truth struck home. That tiny fire, that steady gaze, that tough as a lighter knot old horse was living for the Cause too! "What's his name?" I asked.

"It started out as Corporal," the captain said, patting him on the neck. "But he did such a good job, never complaining, never asking for leave, never whining about his pay, that me and the boys promoted him to Sergeant awhile back. I don't know if it was the right thing to do or not. He got mighty sassy with a few of the boys, bossing them around and stuff. Finally, since I couldn't afford to

59

be a man short, I sent him up the road to see if he could find out anything. Stayed gone six months. When he got back he had a big smile on his face but he didn't know any more about the war than he did before he left." I didn't like the horse, even if his heart was in the right place. It was time to change the subject.

"Don't you men miss your families?" It was a sad question to ask.

"Hell, yes. We miss our families. We all want to go home and see everybody, but if we leave, a Yankee might come down this road, and we wouldn't be doing our duty!"

"But don't you miss your wives and sweethearts? You have no women here, don't you crave some feminine companionship? This is a hard life here, don't you miss the gentle sex?"

He studied the question for a moment. "You know, that question came up a few years back. We all remembered we used to chase girls when we were young sprouts back home," he replied, "but now, none of us can remember why!"

It was getting darker by the minute. I had to get going or I wouldn't make it out of the swamp while it was still light. I wanted to leave these valiant souls with something to be proud of.

"Have you men done a good job here?" It was the right question to ask.

Every proud old face turned toward me, defiance in every wrinkle. It was the sergeant that answered.

"You ain't known of any Yankees that ever came down this road have you?"

"No I ain't," I answered him truthfully. "Well then," he said.

I hated to leave them, but I had to go. I walked on out of the woods to the highway and got a ride back to town. The next day Buster and I came down the river to get the boat, and it took awhile before we could find it.

"This the road you walked out on last night?" Buster asked, pointing to the Charleston Highway. "Ain't much to it, I'm surprised you were able to see it from the river."

"Things ain't always what they seem," I answered, in a hurry to get out of there. I didn't want anyone else to see what I had seen.

We tied the new boat on and headed for Boogie Bear's.

Valentines Day, 1952

*It was an exciting time all right, and it really
didn't have a clear cut ending, but a couple
of people grew up some that day. All I know
is I lost one of my best friends forever.*

There are three Valentine Days that stand out in my
mind. One, and certainly the less important of the
three, was the famous St. Valentine's Day massacre that
happened in Chicago back during prohibition. I wasn't there,
but I understand it was a bloody mess.

The second, and certainly the most important to me, was
in 1956, and was the day that my future wife and I started going
steady. Gave her my class ring to wear either around her neck
on a chain or with a big glob of adhesive tape on her finger. She
wore it until I gave her an engagement ring, which women
seem to put more store in, so she gave the lesser article back
to me. I lost it a couple of months later. She still has the
engagement ring.

But it's the third Valentine's Day that I want to tell you
about. I was there for this one, and it occurred in Miss Werner's
seventh grade class in 1952.

It was one of the most exciting days of my life, and I have

been in two banks while they were being held up (I was not a participant), witnessed three shootings in which two men were killed, been in two car wrecks and was in attendance in the same school two years later when a certain young lady stood on her head while wearing a dress for about a minute and a half.

First I have to give you some background in case there is a young person reading these words. You must understand that ideas and attitudes of seventh grade students in the fifties were not the same as today; we weren't nearly so worldly as you cats, there was no television, no drugs, no smart-mouthing to teachers or parents, and certainly we didn't seem to grow up as fast back then.

It was a difficult age, twelve or thirteen; the boys knew there were girls over there and they were different, but we weren't ready yet. We sort of hung together, hoping we would be noticed but that nothing would come of it.

The girls on the other hand were another matter. Something was happening to them. A perfectly deadly marble shooter a year ago would now cry at the drop of a hat, and every single one of them were now soooo emotional. Giggle, giggle, giggle then for no reason at all – – tears. Thank God for hunting, fishing, shooting marbles and playing ball.

Miss Werner was a very good teacher, and I always liked her, but it seemed she had also developed a problem. She had been divorced four or five years and that year a new, unattached gentleman principal was assigned to our school. The two of them hit it off right away, and it seemed Miss Werner spent more time down in the principal's office than she did in our classroom.

Now for the star players in our little drama.

First, the male lead. Snake. Every single kid in that little class had started to school together in the first grade, except Harry Leroy Railey. Alias Snake.

Snake came to us in the fifth grade from up north somewhere, around Macon. Snake was my pal, we did all sort of fun things together. A girl's name had never crossed either of our lips. All of the boys in the school respected Snake, because that sucker was a fighter. He never went looking for trouble, but he never backed off from it, either. However, after the first few weeks Snake never had to fight anybody, because all the boys had tried him on for size. That was Snake. Fun to be with, never bothered anybody, easy going, but you better not mess with him.

Our other star was Barbara Jean Calhoun. Barbara Jean was the tallest person in our class, the meanest person I have ever seen, and the toughest fighter that ever lived. This was a girl that loved conflict. I had personally been in two fights with this evil little bitch; once in the second grade, where she attacked me with a series of overhand slaps and beat the crap out of me; and again in the fifth, where I did much better, but she finally got me down on the ground and beat the crap out of me again. I steered a wide path around Barbara Jean. There was no girl in the world a match for Barbara Jean, and I can guarantee you I didn't know a single boy that wanted to try her on for size either.

In fact, her older brother, who was a real bully himself, was careful what he said to Barbara Jean. Barbara Jean lived to kick somebody's butt. And she didn't care if it was his.

As much as all the boys hated this thirteen-year-old girl from hell, looking back on it now I realize she really did have some good qualities. She was an "A" student. That's the only grade she ever made in her whole life. I saw her make 98 on a test once and she wanted to cry so bad she could hardly hold it back. But she did.

She must have had a strong mothering instinct, because she looked after those other girls like an old hen. If something bad happened to one of them, they didn't go to the teacher, they went to Barbara Jean. If Barbara Jean couldn't handle it, she went with the girl to the teacher and explained the problem.

She also was the only girl to play tackle football with us. She could run like the wind, and was a sure tackler. The team that had Barbara Jean would always win. She gave no quarter and wanted none.

Now we are ready for the big event.

When we were smaller, say grades one through four, everyone in the class gave Valentines to everybody else. Boys and girls. Then along about the fifth grade the boys quit giving Valentines to other boys, and just a few to certain girls. Then it quit altogether. I don't know what the girls did. I guess they gave them to each other.

About mid-morning of the day in question Miss Werner told us to read a certain chapter in a book and then she split, but we all knew where she went. We sat still for a few minutes, then a tiny little girl's voice said, "Snake gave Margaret a Valentine."

It was a tiny little voice, but everyone in the room heard it.

Snake was mortified. "No I didn't," he protested, but I have to admit, I thought he might have. Had I been a little more brave I know I would have. We might have been little shavers, and not a boy in that room would have ever admitted it, but Margaret Primrose was a little fox!

We began teasing Snake. The onslaught continued through the lunch period, and when Miss Werner left the room that afternoon poor Snake really caught it. It was more than he could take. He jumped up, ran around to the girls' side of the room and confronted Margaret in front of her desk.

"You tell them I didn't give you a Valentine!" he demanded.

Margaret looked up, but she didn't say anything. She didn't

have to. Barbara Jean was coming down the aisle, and she had fire in her eye!

Suddenly, Valentine's Day in the Year of our Lord nineteen hundred and fifty two was getting very interesting.

Barbara Jean put her nose about a millimeter from Snake's nose. They were just about the same height, Barbara Jean just a little taller.

She said it cool and slow.

"I'm gonna slap the snot out of you, boy...." there was lightening shooting out of every syllable.

I have heard that expression many times in my life. It was always said by a girl from the country, and what it means is you better quit whatever it is that you are doing. It could mean you have your

hand where it shouldn't be, or you are looking where you shouldn't look, or whatever. If you don't comply, and quickly, the conquences are you are going to get a real slobber-nocker of a slap. And I don't mean a little patty cake either.

Snake was a fighting man, and he was extremely upset, but he had sense enough to know he didn't want to fight Barbara Jean. He turned his back to Barbara Jean and started walking off. "Yau'll better leave me alone," he said.

It wasn't good enough. Barbara Jean slapped him in the back of the head, hard. He kept walking. Not a person in that classroom blamed him, he was in a situation where he couldn't win.

Barbara Jean wasn't finished. She rushed after him, and slapped him again, and I mean she laid the wood to the back of his head. That did it. Snake was a pretty good-sized boy., standing about five-eight and weighing about a hundred and twenty pounds, wiry and strong. He whirled around and hit Barbara Jean flush in the face with his fist, and he had everything he had behind it.

Pow! I can still hear that punch landing on that girl's face today. It was a conflict ending punch if ever there was one, and Barbara Jean dropped like a sack of potatoes. And she stayed down. That is, for about a second. She came off that floor with her jaw set and fire crackin', and launched into Snake with everything she had.

Nothing could stand up under that onslaught. She was biting, scratching and slapping, all the girl things, but about every third launch was a fist, and she was landing with everything.

They were on the side of the room where the blackboards were, which ran from the front all the way to the back. Snake was giving ground, but he was swinging at her as hard as he could. The fight started just about at the end of the first blackboard, and when they got just about in the middle of the two boards Snake landed another solid punch.

Pow! Barbara Jean dropped like a rock, and while she was down Snake kicked her as hard as he could in the ribs. Up she came, and it was hell to pay – !

The girl from hell.

Snake was fighting for his life now, and he was truly a tough customer. Barbara Jean had forced him now almost to the end of the second blackboard, but he was throwing punches as fast as he could. Some were landing, but they had no affect on Barbara Jean. Then everything seemed to start moving in slow motion, I saw Snake's right hand come back as far as he could reach, and he lashed out at her. His fist landed high on her cheekbone, and I swear, it looked like she hit the floor shoulder blades first.

Then Miss Werner opened the door and walked into the room.

Barbara Jean had risen to a sitting position but was still on the floor. Snake was standing over her, his fists balled up, and what a sight he was. His nose was bleeding, his lip was cut, he had been bitten many times, there was a nasty cut over his eye and there wasn't a place on his face, neck, arms or head that hadn't been scratched. And his shirt was in shreds.

Miss Werner ran up to Snake and slapped him as hard as she could right in the middle of the chest. He never said a word, just turned and walked out the door. I never saw him again.

His parents sent him away to school, and two months later they moved to Alabama. I often wondered whatever came of Old Snake.

We'll never know if Barbara Jean would have gotten up that third time, or who won the fight. We talked about it for months. But I'll tell you what we did know. After that day, and forever more, Barbara Jean was a changed person. No more fighting, no more bullying. She went on to become a star basketball player in high school, and continued to make A's. Last I heard she had two children and was an eye surgeon in Atlanta.

the Doctor's Bass

Some people will do anything to reach their goal, but we all have to be careful not to give up on a good plan too soon. Some plans just take longer to reach fruition.

The good doctor was, is, and probably always will be an incurable bass fisherman. Like some people who can't get enough liquor, women or groceries, the doctor is hooked on bass fishing. He fishes on top, on the bottom, and in between. Big water, little water, fast, still, clear, muddy – – he tries them all. Mention a new lure, and he has already tried it. Talk about an article on the subject in an obscure magazine, and he has already read it, tried its suggestions and written to the editor about what he found out.

He only wants one thing out of life, but that one thing has always eluded him – – a trophy bass for his den wall.

The doctor has caught literally thousands of bass, but he has never reached his goal, and since he is also something of a perfectionist he has never had a bass mounted. "I'll never mount one until I catch a ten-pounder," he said often enough, and he meant it.

70

But as they tend to do, the years kept rolling by, and try as hard as he might, the magic goal was never reached. The spot in his new house built especially to surround his trophy fish remained bare.

One afternoon on his way to Bankers Pond, a favorite old mill near his house, he noticed a little slough about a hundred feet from the pond. No more than thirty feet in diameter, it was actually more like a big hole, but it was full of water and as far as he could tell it was several feet deep. Although it was just off the road, it was pretty well hidden and he had never noticed it before. It's only distinguishing characteristic was an old tree trunk running into the water at a low angle, making a natural footbridge almost halfway across.

He had almost walked on by the place before the idea hit him. He stood in the road thinking a minute, and a fiendish smile slowly spread across his face. He would catch a bass, put it in the hole, feed it every day, and catch it out when it reached trophy size!

No one would ever know, but if they did, so what? Everything would be on the up and up. When you catch a big bass, you catch a big bass. For all any- one would know, that fish had

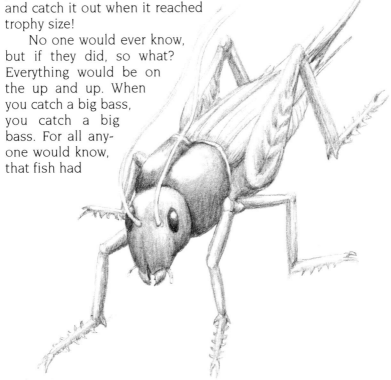

71

always been in that hole. With visions of the mighty bass hanging on his wall, he shoved off onto Bankers Pond, anxious to catch the fish that would one day be his braggin' piece.

Alas, his fishing skill ran to form. He wanted to put a five-pounder or better in that hole, but all he could catch that day was one runty little fish that weighed about a pound. By night-fall his enthusiasm had dimmed somewhat, like most red hot ideas do once they settle a bit, and he was tired, but on impulse he went ahead and tossed the little bass into the hole.

"Trophy bass, go to trophy hole," he chanted three times, recalling a technique for finding lost marbles.

In the following weeks, he stopped by the trophy hole every time he visited Bankers Pond, and several times he caught a few minnows and released them in the little place. But catching minnows was sometimes hard work and it cut down on his fishing time, so his visits to the trophy hole gradually became less frequent. Besides, there was no sign of trophy bass. "Must have died," he thought, and went on his way.

Weeks, months, even years went by. A couple of babies were born, his practice grew, he became active in community affairs and the time spent casting for his den-wall bass was less, but he always retained the dream. One Sunday morning, he took his kids to Bankers Pond. Armed with a couple of poles and a box of crickets, they sat lazily in the sun. Stretched out on the grass, the doctor suddenly thought about Trophy Pond. "I wonder if it's still over there," he thought, and he walked back to look.

It was there all right, still the same size, the same tree running down into the water, the same – – suddenly there was a powerful flash of light and movement, and near the tree trunk the most monstrous bass the doctor had ever seen struck something on the surface! The strike was so powerful it almost scared the doctor out of his wits! It took him several minutes to regain his composure, then he was running back to the car for his casting rod.

It was Trophy Bass in Trophy Pond! The little devil had made it! He felt like he had been struck with a bolt of lightning composed of every good thing that had ever happened to him!

72

He grabbed the first top-water plug he saw in his tackle box, tied it on his line and ran back to Trophy Pond, stopping a little short to creep silently up to its edge.

All was quiet.

On one knee, keeping a low profile, he flipped the plug against the tree trunk. It bounced off and landed in the water with a little splat. His heart was pounding as he waited, and seconds later, he gave the plug a little twitch. The sun was shining through the water, and he actually saw the mighty fish surge upward from the depths and slam into the plug. It wasn't the fool-around-namby-pamby bump of a fish at the bottom of the social scale, it was a mighty, gut-wrenching explosion of a strike, terrifying every living creature that observed it.

He reared back and set the hook, but he wasn't prepared for the strength of the huge bass at the other end of his line. The fish powered its way under the tree and thrashed around for a few seconds, then a sinking feeling flowed down the rod and into his heart – – the fish was hung up! He could still feel the fish on the line, but it was hung up – – solid.

Now there was no way the doctor was going to let that fish get away. He had been looking for it all his life, and now that he had it on the end of his line in a little hole, he wasn't going to let it get away!

He pulled off his shoes and stepped into the green water. It was about knee deep, and the bottom seemed firm enough. He waded toward the tree, and was just about there when suddenly the bottom changed, and he sank up to his armpits in soft ooze. All the excitement had suddenly turned dangerous, and he could have been drowning in another few seconds, but his thoughts still were on Trophy Bass.

Suddenly the fish made a mighty jump on the other side of the tree, and landed on the tree trunk just inches from the doctor's nose. For seconds that must have seemed like an eternity, the good doctor and Trophy Bass were eyeball to eyeball!

"As I looked at that fish, my whole life flashed in front of me," the doctor said later. "But I don't know if that was because of the fish or the fact that I was about to drown."

Trophy Bass had seen enough. It gave another lunge, tore the hook loose, and disappeared into the green water.

The doctor grabbed the tree trunk and slowly pulled himself to the bank. He had lost the fish, but he didn't feel too badly about it, because he knew it was there, and he'd simply catch it later. Besides, he was alive. And if he had drowned in that little hole, how would his wife ever have explained it?

However, Trophy Bass was a little shy about dating the doctor again. For the next six months he fished for Trophy Bass every way he knew. Early. Late. At night. Plastic worms. Live minnows. Eels. Nothing worked. In fact, he never saw a sign of the fish. "Must have died," he finally decided, and went on his way.

As many of us do in such matters, the doctor finally lowered his standards. He caught a nice eight-pound bass several months later, and rather proud, took it to the local taxidermist. He had the bass wrapped in some newspapers, and was unwrapping it when a kid came in carrying an old styrofoam cooler.

The doctor stood transfixed as the kid took the lid off the cooler and revealed the biggest bass anybody had ever seen. "I didn't know they got that big," the taxidermist said. It had to be a record of some kind.

"My God," the doctor asked, "where did you get such a fish?"

"It's kind of funny," the boy said, "I was coming from Bankers Pond when I heard a sloshing sound over behind some bushes. I looked and there was a hole full of water. Wasn't bigger'n nothing'. I put a cricket on and threw it in there and this is what I caught. Fished for an hour after that and never got another bite."

Pale and weak, the doctor wrapped the papers around his fish, which the boy's bass would have eaten for a snack, and eased quietly out the door.

(Told by Dr. Saied Ameen of Camden, South Carolina while we were sitting in the truck waiting for the rain to quit.)

74

the Golden Goddess

A girl like this one only comes along once in a lifetime, but how does a guy get her to notice him among all those guys at the beach? It helps to be prepared. Especially if you have a trained great white shark.

h, summer.

Blows there a sweeter wind? I think not.

My friend Everett and I both reached the magic age of sixteen at just about the same time. Magic because that was the year in which every peckerhead could get his drivers license.

Growing up in a small town I had been driving since I was about twelve, but I couldn't go outside of town nor could I get on the highway. Our town cop could care less if I drove, but a state trooper probably wouldn't know any better and write me a ticket.

But now, after all that time, both of us were legal. One just didn't get his license and forget about it, we had to take a celebration trip. And for months we had been planning a wonderful excursion that would introduce us to girls from all over the country.

When school was out we would drive to Jacksonville Beach, Florida, where we would spend approximately two weeks soaking up the rays in the arms of beautiful girls, whom we knew would be waiting for us and who would find us utterly charming, ruggedly handsome and irresistible.

By limiting ourselves almost to the bare necessities of life we had managed to save forty dollars. This, we figured, would be plenty enough for two weeks, since after the first day or two we would be living with various females, moving only when we began to tire of their company.

Everett's older brother was in the Navy, and being a regular sort of guy had loaned us his car. It helped that the brother was on a six-month cruise, because by the time he got back we would have long since returned from Florida and he would never know anything about it. It was a black forty-nine Chevy coupe. We alternated driving it ninety-six miles per hour, which was as fast as it would go, all the way to Jacksonville.

Before we left my Grandad had given me his Standard Oil credit card. "For emergencies only."

"If you get down there and find you can't get home, and you can't think of any other way, then use the card," he said. I told him I would take it, but I was sure it wouldn't be needed, but to make him feel better I'd put it in my billfold.

The night before we left I was packing my duffel bag and I saw something that literally doubled me over with laughter. It was my old shark fin. When I was about twelve I had seen it advertised in a magazine. About three bucks. It was made to look like the fin of a great white shark. It ran on two size "D" flashlight batteries and had a little propeller which would push it through the water about as fast as most people would think a shark would swim when looking for something to eat. Of course, you couldn't see that part. When it was in the water all you could see was the fin part.

I remember how disappointed I was when it arrived, because it was painted a bright red. I fixed that, though. I spray-painted it black, let it dry, then laid a burlap sack over it and sprayed it again, this time with gray paint. Enough of the gray came through to give it a slight pattern, like a shark would have on his fin.

I tested it at a Sunday-school swim party at Kinchafonee Creek. When the old swimming hole was full of about fifty sinners, I turned Blacky-shark on and let him meander out across the multitudes. You know that part about Jesus walking on the water in the Bible? I can guarantee you there ain't a member of that class that doubts it happened, because they saw some plain folks do it that day!

In fact, my Sunday school teacher was a mean old lady named Mrs. Tuggle. She was about up to her boobs when she looked about and saw Blacky-shark coming toward her. Claimed she wrenched her back climbing up that muddy bank. She caught me though, and shook me so hard my teeth rattled. Called me a mean-spirited, ungrateful little heathen.

Of course, Mrs. Tuggle and about fifteen other people called my Grandparents and told them what I had done. When I explained to my Grandad exactly how it happened, he laughed so hard he dropped his glasses. "Put that thing away and I don't want to ever see it again!," he said. And I did.

Until now.

On impulse I threw it in my duffel. Maybe one of the girls will find it amusing, I thought.

When we first got to Jacksonville Beach things were a little slow. Oh, there were a lot of girls there all right, but it seems they were distracted or something and didn't notice us. Our plans were that if we weren't taken in by some beautiful girls on the first day, we would sleep on the beach and give them another chance on day two.

We were eating all our meals at a little pancake house across the road from the beach. We could get a big stack of pancakes there for seventy-nine cents, and that's all we ate. We were getting tired of pancakes, but it matched our budget. One morning we were going inside when I noticed the headline on the newspaper – – "Girl killed by shark at Daytona Beach!"

Now Daytona Beach is not too far south of Jacksonville Beach, and everyone was extremely concerned. In fact, hardly anyone went swimming that day, but soon it was forgotten.

Sleeping on the beach is kinda grimey and after three or four days of that crap it started getting old, so we broke down and rented a little house, consisting of a bedroom, bath and little screened porch. Its one redeeming factor was it sat right on the beach. If you jumped off our porch, you landed on the beach. Twenty dollars a week. Perfect.

Our porch commanded a view of the beach in both directions. We could sit here at our leisure, spot a likely group of girls, make our plans, then move out to be discovered. I was just explaining to Everett how it was going to work, when a vision appeared.

She was walking along the beach, south to north. Right across our bow. Thirty feet away. There are no words in the English language to describe how beautiful that girl was. At that time, all the boys thought Brigitte Bardot had the greatest body anyone had ever seen. This girl made Brigitte look like a twelve-year-old!

She was blond, but not a bright blonde. Sort of a dishwater

blond. A golden tan, beautiful teeth, blue eyes that just flashed. I guessed she was about two years older than me and Everett. About eighteen, and so far out of our league we might as well have been billy goats!

There were actually several guys following her down the beach, trying to talk to her, but all she would do was look at them and smile, toss her head and keep walking. All she had to do to draw a crowd was to walk out on the beach!

Neither Everett nor I spoke until she was out of sight. We had been struck dumb. Excuse me. Dumber. We both agreed, we had never in our whole lives seen a girl like that. A girl to dream about.

The beach was fun in the daytime, but at night is when the action really begins. There was a long pier that ran several hundred feet out into the ocean, and at the end of it was a giant dance floor and nifty music. It was Everett's briar patch. If there had ever been a person made for this type of environment, it was Everett. He was a smooth talker and a great dancer. Naturally extroverted, he was in his element. Everett would meet the girls, and then introduce them to me. If there were only two, and one of them looked like a gump, guess which one I got.

"There's a couple over there," Everett would say, "yours doesn't look so good but look at mine!"

I didn't care. We were having a ball. We were in the middle of the game one night out

on the pier when suddenly, out on the dance floor, walked the Golden Goddess. She was wearing a tight white skirt, and every male eye in the place was fixed on her. She began dancing with a tall, good looking guy that looked like some sort of foreigner. He had black hair, all slicked back on the sides like a movie star. He also had a great tan, pearly-white teeth and dimples. The girls around me were about to swoon.

"He's an I-talian," one of the girls near me said.

To hell with the I-talian, I thought, he's dancing with my girl and I've got to figure out what I'm going to do about it. It wasn't going to be easy. That guy was about twenty-five, had the self assurance of a cat-burglar and the two of them hadn't taken their eyes off each other all night.

They soon left, arm in arm, looking deeply into each other's eyes.

When we got home that night I told Everett I couldn't believe it, a great-looking southern girl like that keeping time with a Yankee I-talian.

"That guy ain't a Yankee," Everett said, "he's from Memphis."

"An I-talian from Memphis? Ain't no I-talians in Memphis," I told him. I just couldn't believe it.

"Yes , it is, " he said. "I met one of his friends."

I told Everett that I intended to meet that girl, take her away from the fake-Yankee and make her mine. He laughed himself to sleep.

I lay awake in the dark, trying to think of a plan of action that would somehow gain me access to the Golden Goddess. I reasoned that if somehow she could get to know me, surely she would soon realize that all the other guys she had ever known were second-rate, and that I was the prize of all prizes.

But I couldn't think of a single thing to do.

The next afternoon Everett had gone off with one of the girls he met, and I was dozing on the porch and dreaming of the Golden Goddess. Bored, soon I walked down to the water and out about knee-deep, and was look-ing toward France when I heard a giggle behind me.

I turned around, and it was the Golden Goddess and the Memphis I-talian, arm in arm, eyes locked, wading into the surf.

He picked her up, and waded further out, until they were in a little over his waist, where they looked in each other's eyes and bobbed up and down in the waves.

It was sickening. I was so jealous I swore to myself I would never eat another pizza in my life. Then, out of the blue, like a bolt from heaven – – I thought of Blackie-shark.

"Oh, Lord," I prayed," please let them stay just where they are for a little longer." I walked as fast as I could without attracting attention to the little house, and there was Blackie-shark, nestled in his little bed in my duffel bag, awaiting the call.

They were still there when I came out; he had her cradled in his arms, nibbling on her ear as they gently bobbed up and down.

"I'm gonna put a stop to all that biting crap," I thought as I hurried down to the water's edge. I had Blackie-shark under my arm, tight against my body, and fortunately, there was no one else close by. I waded out about waist deep, careful to keep Blackie-shark out of sight. It wouldn't have mattered, all they had eyes for was each other.

I aimed Blackie-shark in their general direction and switched him on, then began swimming toward the shore behind them. I swam about thirty or forty feet, then stood up and looked back to see if anything was happening.

What was happening was a great white shark was closing in on two unsuspecting lovers, and they hadn't seen it yet.

There was an ear piercing scream. The Golden Goddess had seen Blackie. The Memphis I-talian looked up at Blackie and didn't say a word. He just dropped the Goddess and went for the beach like a bulldozer. I guess she went all the way to the bottom, I don't know, but I do know that when I got to her side her suntan was gone, and she was white as a sheet!

"Don't move," I commanded her in the deepest voice I could muster, "it's movement they go after – – stay here and I'll see if I can't change his evil mind!"

Blackie was swimming figure eights about ten feet away.

There are a lot of things I can't do. Like dance, for instance.

Or play golf. But I can stay underwater forever. The length of the pool and back, no sweat. I disappeared under the water and headed for Blackie.

When I got under the great white shark I positioned my body just right, then snatched the fin under the water, at the same time kicking and trashing on the surface like the confrontation of the ages was taking place. After about thirty seconds I went to the bottom and drove Blackie into the sand as hard and as deep as I could, then came up out of the water like a rocket.

"Wow, that was a tough one," I said as I wiped my brow with my forearm.

"What happened?, she said in a tiny little voice.

Deep voice. "Their noses are very sensitive. I finally managed to get him where I could bend his nose back and hurt him plenty. He won't come around here again!"

She looked like she was about to faint. I wrapped my arms around her and led her to the beach. A crowd of people had gathered but none of them were going in the water to help.

Feels real good, I was thinking as I hugged her to shore. Someone produced a beach chair and a towel, and a lady wiped her face. Something had scared the hell out of that girl.

She looked up at me. "What's your name?"

I told her. It didn't seem to register.

"I'm staying in that little house, there," and I pointed to it. She looked at me like she wanted to say something, then looked at the little house, smiled weakly, and allowed herself to be led away.

It was all over, and I didn't know if I had done any good or not. At least the Memphis I-talian had been exposed for what he was. Everett got back about six.

"You hear anything about a shark attack on this end of the beach today?" he asked. I told him I had not.

"Everybody's talking about a girl being attacked by a shark, and some guy swam out and rescued her, just like Tarzan."

"Really?"

There was a knock on the door. I opened the screen , and there stood the Golden Goddess, resplendent in a light blue dress. There were two older people with her, I assumed they were her parents. "I'm sorry," she said, "I don't remember your name." Before I could say anything, she turned to the gentleman with her. "Daddy, this is the very brave young man that saved my life today."

"I'm Dr. Murphy," he said as he extended his hand. "We want to thank you for what you did. We are eternally grateful."

I explained that it really wasn't anything, I was just glad I was there in time of need. Turns out Dr. Murphy was a surgeon in Waycross, Georgia. He said they lived on a farm just on the outside of town, and they sure would appreciate it if we would stop by and visit them on our way home.

They invited Everett and me out to dinner with them, an invitation we gladly accepted, as we both had had it with the pancakes. I sat next to the Golden Goddess while she filled me in on the details of her life, while I was my usual amusing, witty, debonair self.

On the way back to our little house, they told us they were leaving for Waycross that very night, because they had all been so terrified at what almost happened they didn't want to see another ocean.

They dropped us off, her mother gave me a big hug, and after assurances we would visit them in Waycross, they motored away.

"It didn't work, " I thought as we went inside. "I lost her anyway. "

"What are you looking so glum about?" Everett asked. "It ain't but seventy-four miles from our house to Waycross. And did you see that picture of her little sister?"

Everett had the right idea. But it could never work. She was out of my league the first time I ever saw her, and the last time. I was intimidated by the Goddess.

I tried to find Blackie, but never could. It was a shame, because that little deal was a sure-fire winner.

So if you are ever at Jacksonville Beach, feel around for a little guy stuck in the sand. About 30 feet out. Just be careful, you never know when the real thing will show up!

the Chinaberry Militia

*Getting shot with a bullet is bad enough,
but getting shot with a green chinaberry
hurts! Too bad the southern boys didn't find
out sooner, the outcome of the great war
might have been different!*

Some time ago while reading a war story I began to
wonder who were the greatest fighting men in history.
I thought many of you would also like to know, so I
began an exhaustive research program to get at the truth.

I know you understand that this was no small feat, because
there have been fighting men on this earth ever since Adam
discovered what Eve had done to him with the apple.

At this time I am happy to announce that I have finished
my research and my findings are complete. I discovered that
there are essentially four groups of warriors who stand treetop
tall over all others, and although none of them have been victo-
rious all the time, they have won more battles than they lost.

They are, in alphabetical order: the Japanese Samurai
warriors, many of which made up the Kamikaze pilots of the
Second World War; the famed Gurkha warriors of Nepal; the

fierce Cossacks of Russia; and last but not least, any group of South Georgia Rednecks.

Since I'm sure you are knowledgeable about the feats of the first three groups of outstanding soldiers, to save both of us some time I shall devote the remainder of this epistle to the latter group, the hell-raising, backslapping, ear-biting, good ole boys from Georgia below the city of Macon, who come into this world looking for trouble and as a general rule go out the same way, usually after finding it.

In addition to my research, I am eminently qualified to discuss the merits of these fine fellows, having been born and raised among them, and having grown up with the firm conviction that anyone living in Atlanta is a Yankee.

I am firmly convinced that if you took one fellow from each of the four groups I mentioned and put them in a sack and shook them up, there would be heck of a fight, but the redneck would eventually come out of the sack and look for someone to thank for inviting him to the party.

This is not to say that they are not of an agreeable and friendly nature; indeed, some of their greatest fights are among friends. In fact, they are friends because they will oblige each other with a fight now and then and not get mad.

In order to give you the benefit of my research, I shall now relate a few episodes I found securely tucked away in literary journals that tell the true story of these fantastic fighters, so you can see for yourself why I regard them so highly. These shall be related in chronological order.

In the great Civil War of the United States these fantastic soldiers were hardly represented; had they been I'm sure

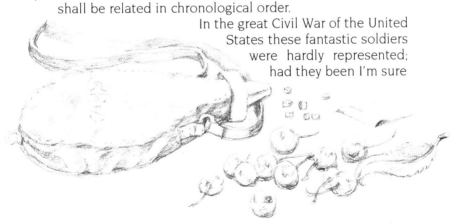

87

the outcome would have
been different. The reason they weren't in
the war until the last was because nobody told
them about it until the last. They thought it was a war
between the big planters' sons and the Yankees and they
weren't invited.

However, when they discovered that anyone who wanted
to could join up and fight Yankees, the northern army had
already captured Atlanta. Undaunted, and praying the war
wouldn't end before they got there, they banded together to
form a little army, trained strenuously for about an hour and a
half, then set out to find the Yankees.

Unfortunately, they didn't know where Atlanta was, and
they walked all the way to Austin, Texas before they realized
they were headed in the wrong direction. There they met a
squad of Mexican banditos who had a rather hard time
explaining that they weren't Yankees, then at their first opportunity the banditos cut and ran for the border, never to return.

The rednecks marched all the way back to Pensacola,
Florida, and still not having found the Yankees, could stand it
no longer and began to fight among themselves. That is their
one drawback. If one or more of them come together, a fight is
gonna start, enemy or not. They chose up sides and fought it
out for three days; the carnage was terrific. Finally someone
volunteered that a lot of good old southern boys were never
gonna get to fight the Yankees if they all died in Florida, so a
ceasefire was called to ponder the problem.

The solution was near at hand, dear reader. Instead of
bullets, the noble warriors would use chinaberries, and while
a green chinaberry would leave a wicked blister when fired
from a .58 caliber meat gun, the recipient would live to fight
another day.

A thirty-minute chinaberry pickin' time was allowed, then

the fight resumed. Friends, you cannot believe what went on along a fifty-mile strip between Tallahassee, Florida and Albany, Georgia for the next four days. Historians still rate it as the greatest battle ever fought. Neither side would give in. Charge and counter charge. It was a skull-splitting, eye-gougin', chinaberry blisterin' of a fight. To this very day, scattered along the battle lines the entire way is a living memorial to this battle, a chinaberry forest so thick a snake can't crawl through it.

Just as the issue was drawing to a final close, a message arrived via mule-back that the Yankees had left the far-off city of Atlanta and were marching on Macon.

Macon!

They all knew where Macon was! The two little armies turned into one big dust cloud, racing pell-mell for Macon. When they arrived, they found the Rebel army fortifying the city for the Yankee attack, but the rednecks had never fought from a defensive position in their life. They marched around the city and headed north, where they collided with 10,000 of Sherman's finest coming down the road. The Yankees had orders to take Macon, then go on down to Andersonville Prison and release the brethren stationed there by the Rebels.

When they saw the Yankees, these newest recruits to the southern cause closed their ranks and charged, each wearing a big grin. For six days the 154 rednecks and 10,000 Yankees fought it out, after which the Yankees decided they didn't really want to go to Macon anyway. They made a left turn and headed for Savannah. The lowdown rascals told the rednecks that Savannah was in New Jersey, so our brave warriors held a victory barbecue and went home the next day.

As a matter of fact, the good Yankee boys in Andersonville Prison weren't liberated until after the war was over. A slight oversight, Sherman claimed.

After the war ended and the troops went home, many northern ladies were puzzled by the strange red welts on their husbands' backsides. Seems most of the rednecks forgot to put the bullets back in their guns, and fought the entire battle with chinaberries!

To this day in South Georgia the good folks there think the South won the war, and the deciding battle was fought just above Macon with chinaberries. I have listened to my own Granddad tell many times how he chased a hundred Yankees all over some unknown mountain with one last chinaberry.

I ran across many such episodes, dear reader, some of which prove our decision to include these noble fellows in such elite company indeed wise.

Of course I'm sure you are familiar with the one time these great soldiers refused to fight. I understand Napoleon offered two hundred rednecks a dollar and a half each if they would whip Russia for him and he could stay in Paris. The two hundred jumped at the chance, and started walking to Russia via Alaska. They walked all the way to Arkansas when a kindred spirit there told them they had neither beer, moonshine, white socks or bib overalls in Russia. Our warriors agreed that money wasn't everything in the world, turned around and went home.

This may have been a dark day in their history, but as recently as the Viet Nam War their spirit again came to the fore. Twenty-eight of their finest volunteered to land in China and whip everything all the way from there to Saigon. The army thought it was an outstanding idea, and were making plans on how they were going to land a flatbed truck in China when the war ended. People in South Georgia say both sides heard about the plan and quit. It was said the noble warriors were going to take a month's supply of chinaberries.

I have also studied these outstanding warriors as individuals. It seems a South Georgia redneck will fight anyone but two people. His father, because if he ever hit his father the old man would be honor bound to kill him, and his mother, because she's the only one who can whip his dad, and she keeps the old man off his back.

I'm glad I was able to bring these facts to you.

(Note: This story first appeared in South Carolina Wildlife Magazine in the late seventies. Not long after it came out I received a photograph from Michigan of an old man with his pants down, revealing a large red welt about the size of a half dollar on his left cheek. The guy who sent it said it was his great grandfather, and the picture had been taken around the turn of the century. He said the old man told him that he had gotten it in a fight in Georgia "when the Rebels cheated and started shooting some sort of berry at them ")

the Great Nauga Project

*The federal government works in wonderful
and mysterious ways, but it's always with
mine and your money. We've got about ten
times more government than we need,
but as this story emphasizes, they are
doing some very important work.*

A while back, long about the first of October or so, I had correctly judged myself to be entirely devoid of self-discipline. I frequently over indulged in things fun and pleasurable, such as ice cream floats, commonly called "flips" at my house, and I knew if I didn't do something, and do it quickly, I could very well be lost to sin forever.

In order to convince everyone (i.e. my wife) that I did indeed have some self control I told her I would arise at the ungodly hour of four a.m. and without breakfast, drive twenty miles, walk into the woods and climb a tree. I would further handicap myself by carrying a rifle, scope and tree stand. I would do this before day, and I would remain in said tree motionless and soundless for three hours.

"To do something like that takes self discipline and control, a sacrifice of creature comfort, and most certainly expresses a desire to improve," I assured her. She remained unaffected, and without comment carried on with her household chores.

Everything went as planned the following morning. I arrived on time and found the tree I had spotted a week earlier. I climbed to about fifteen feet and began my wait for a certain big buck that had been frequenting the area.

He must not have received the message, because he never showed up and around ten a.m. I was ready to give it up. Just as I was tying a string on my rifle to let it down, I heard a noise. Something was coming through the woods, and it was something big. However, I quickly realized that it had to be human, because it never stopped, as deer do, but continued without pause. Soon two men came into view, carrying a strange-looking box. They came toward me, and in fact, walked right up under the tree I was in and sat down on the box to rest.

Seldom is a person afforded an opportunity of this magnitude. A soul could live a hundred years and not get two guys, way down in the deep, dark woods, perhaps in the lair of monsters, to sit down and relax like guppies scarcely ten feet away, never knowing there was another person in ten miles.

Quickly my computer-like mind began going over the many types of screams I could use to scare the hell out of them. Finally deciding on the old-fashioned tried-and-true gut-shot panther, I let them have my best. It starts out as a low growl and ends up as a high-pitched scream.

United States Department of Agriculture

Nauga Research

Later we found that both of them had jumped about fifty feet before making a track, and then only one before they hit the creek. It was so funny I couldn't laugh it all up then, but had to store it up and laugh on it some later. I had to get down out of the tree and fall off the box on the ground and laugh. You should have seen those suckers tippe-toeing out from under that tree!

By the time they got back I was plumb wore out, but being pretty good fellows they even helped me laugh on it some. They both had on uniforms, and their shoulder patches identified them as being employed by the U. S. Department of Agriculture.

They introduced themselves as Bernard Nauch and Billy Nettles Goforth, researchers with the department. I was dying to know what they were up to and I asked them about the weird-looking box.

"Actually," Billy said, "we are asked that question a lot. This is a nauga trap."

I hated to appear stupid while talking to representatives of the U. S. Government, but I had never heard of a nauga, and I asked him what one was.

"That's another question we get from time to time," Bernard said. "A nauga is a little animal that lives in the woods in the Southeastern United States. Very fast, very smart, and very scarce. Have you ever been in a doctor's office?"

I assured him that I had.

"Then you probably have seen sofas and chairs covered with naugahide. Many coats and other articles of clothing are also made from their hides; they are extremely valuable little animals."

I was beginning to feel like I had just come in to the middle of a movie. A bad movie. "Why are you fellows doing research on them?"

"Well," Billy said, "they've been used so much that the department began to worry about their future. You know there is such a thing as over-exploitation of a species, and part of our job is to protect all commercial species of wildlife."

"Is it just the two of you working on this project?" I had a feeling there was more to know.

"Heck no," he said. "We have a complete research center in town. We have our own building and everything. In fact, in this, our second year of research, we have now installed a complete computer center to handle the data we are collecting."

I told them I was extremely interested in the project and would like to visit their main office sometime. "Sure," he said, we're going there now, just as soon as we finish setting this trap. Why don't you just follow us back to Columbia?"

They raised the door of the box, put in the bait – – an evil smelling gob of goo – – set the trigger and away we went. On the way to town I asked if they had ever caught a nauga. They said they had not, that they had a hard time developing a trap. The nauga was so fast he got out every time. But technology is wonderful, they not only had a new trap now, but also new bait, and hopes were high.

Their main office was a tall white building of seven or eight stories, and was easily identified by the large steel and concrete sign out front – – "United States Department of Agriculture-Nauga Research." It was one of the ugliest buildings I have ever seen. It ranks right up there with Baptist Hospital in Columbia and the new Richland County Public Library, which are two world class uglies.

Inside it was easy to see that this was a very important place. People were walking fast up and down the halls, secretaries were busy typing, and executives were hurrying to important meetings. Important research papers were being printed and future budgets were being prepared.

I asked if I could meet the head man, and, after a short wait, was told he could work me into his schedule for five minutes. While I was waiting, I asked a secretary what she was typing.

"A letter," she replied with a condescending smile.

"To whom?" I asked, displaying superior breeding and three years spent in freshman English.

"To Mr. Heinie, director of Procurement and Conventionalism, two doors down."

I asked why she didn't just walk over and tell him instead of writing a letter; she looked at me like I was a fool, then said it was official government business.

95

Soon I was ushered into the office of Mr. Robert James Bigelow Tutrel, the director of the entire project.

"I think there is something you ought to know..." I began to say, but was interrupted by an aide who told Mr. Tutrel the new budget of $50 million dollars had been approved by Washington. Tutrel was so excited he excused himself to call ten Democratic congressmen to give his personal thanks for their help. Then he told me all about how he could hire one hundred more government employees and about how his cost-benefit ratio was looking better all the time.

"But there ain't no such thing as a...," I began to say, but we were interrupted again by an aide, who informed Mr. Tutrel that his plane was now ready for the trip to Monte Carlo with the ten congressmen. "We've got to see how the nauga is faring in a depressed environment," he explained as he rushed out.

As I walked out through the busy government employees, I overheard a conversation: "I understand some mean old Southerners," one was saying, "used to smuggle naugas north in the false bottom of watermelon trucks. The melons would drown out their little cries of agony."

It was too much, and I literally ran for the first door I saw. As I ran out into the sunshine, there was

an old swamp rat unloading several crates with the words "Official Nauga Bait" stenciled on the side.

I confronted him eyeball to eyeball. "You ain't no federal employee. You know better than this. Why are you party to such waste?"

"Listen, young fellow," he said, "I was minding my own business when two city fellers came through the swamp and asked me if I knew anything about naugas. Thought they were pulling my leg. Told them I used to trap them for a living. They asked how I did it and I told them the bait was the secret. Been selling them nauga bait at $100 a pound ever since. You keep quiet, and when I die, I'll leave the business to you."

As I walked through the gate, I couldn't help thinking how fortunate we were that our tax money could go to such a good cause.

Cold Kisses

*If you cheat, fate will have it in for you, and
you will surely lose in the end. Maybe we would
all be better off without so much plotting and
scheming and just let life take its normal course.*

The most desirable girl in our school was Margaret
Primrose. No other girl was even close. She was beautiful,
sexy, soft and dreamy. She was also virtually engaged to
this creep who went to Furman University, who played tight
end on the football team and thought he was hot stuff. Mere
mortals need not apply.

I did not like this particular arrangement. I wanted
Margaret to be mine. I had been wanting Margaret since about
the sixth grade, soon as I got old enough to realize what a foxy
little babe Margaret was.

Margaret was not only not interested in me, she wasn't
interested in anyone except the tight end creep, and it had
been that way virtually for years. And for years I had been
secretly frustrated, challenged, and annually defeated by this
insane, perfectly stupid facination that Margaret had for this guy.

The year that Margaret and I were seniors in high school, I

realized that time was running out, and something had to be done, or my dream of the luscious Margaret would soon be gone forever. I made a list of the pros and cons. What were my advantages, what were his.

His advantages were he was rich, good looking, a big man on campus, star on the football team, soon would be going to medical school and he had a bright future. Also, Margaret thought he was some kind of God, he drove a new convertible, had a lot of trendy things to say and could dance like hell.

So much for the creep.

Now how did I stack up? I had an old Ford pickup held together with baling wire and missing the glass on the right side, could paddle a boat, knew where the bream always bedded in the spring, could hit what I was shooting at most of the time, was cordially disliked by my coach and most of the teachers in school, which should give me some sympathy points, and was a big man on campus, my campus, small though it may be.

I just scraped by in school, had absolutely no future and was looked on in disdain by Mr. and Mrs. Primrose.

That could be a plus.

I showed my list to my good buddy Buster. "My God, man, if you can't snake a girl away from a guy who ain't even here, it ain't much to you." Buster had a way with words, but when I thought about it, that had to be the one chink in this creep's armor. Furman University wasn't in South Georgia! He was far away! I was here!

If that is my strongest asset, then I need to apply it liberally, I reasoned. And I did. I positioned myself at Margaret's elbow and didn't get three inches from that girl for the next week.

At first she thought I was some sort of weirdo. But I told her how beautiful she was forty-seven times a day. I carried her books. I bragged on everything she did. And I never said anything bad about the creep.

We had a good basketball team that year, and I thought I was the main reason why. Watching the boys in the ACC today, I know now that I wasn't much, but I thought I was back then. Hot stuff. There were two great benefits to small high school basketball: one, you got to strut your stuff on the court and enjoy playing the game; and two, that long ride back home after the game on that dark, slow school bus, complete with cheerleader or girl basketball player, whose squads rode the same bus we did. The back seat was best, no one could see what was going on back there.

Our team had reached the play-offs, and that Friday we were scheduled to play Vienna for the division championship. If we could win that, we advanced to the state tournament, and absolute glory.

Thursday when Margaret came to school it was apparent she had been crying, and she wouldn't talk to anybody. I thought she was just having a girl thing, but after lunch one of her friends told me she was breaking up with the creep. Said she didn't know why.

Bingo!

I was the man with the plan. And it had worked. Now she was falling free through the air, and I had to get that safety net under her. I got my chance when I saw her in the hall after the next period. "You sure are pretty with red eyes," I said quietly, brushing her hair back. Tender. Sweet.

She looked up at me and smiled. In like Flynn! After all those years, and finally, pure charm had won out! It was time to pop the question. "Say, tomorrow night, on the way back from the game, why don't we share the same seat? I mean, I think you are the greatest girl I've ever seen. I sure would like to hold you close " It was so tender the words wouldn't hardly hold together.

She looked up at me with those beautiful eyes and gave me a little smile. "I think that would be just wonderful," she said.

Cloud nine would not describe the feeling I had. I was much higher up than that. We had basketball practice that afternoon and the coach told us about the other team and made this great motivational speech. However, it didn't motivate me. I was thinking about Margaret. And I continued to think about Margaret all night and the next day.

"It has to be perfect," I told myself. "If something happens to blow this now it could be the end of our relationship. Of course, she could go back to the creep and this will be my only chance with her, so I've got to make the best of it. We have got to get the back seat!"

Here's the way it worked. The girls played first, then the boys. If your date was on the girls team, it helped, because once the boys game started the girls could slip out anytime and claim a good seat on the bus. However, if your date was a cheerleader, you were out of luck, because they had to stay in the gym until the boys game was over. By then, the girl basketball players would have all the best seats. Of course, some of the best looking girls were cheerleaders, so it was a tradeoff.

Margaret was on the basketball team. I explained to her what she had to do. "You slip away from those other girls at halftime of our game, and go out and get the back seat. If you wait any longer, I'm afraid someone will beat us to it. I'm going to be your sweetest dream come true," I told her. Margaret was a real trooper. She said she would. Hot dog!

Vienna was a formidable opponent. They were always tough. Their center was a big guy, six feet five, with a deadly jump shot. He wasn't much of a banger under the board, but

101

he was quick and graceful, and if he got the ball ten or twelve feet from the basket, you could ring it up. He could jump like a kangaroo, straight up, feet together, body straight as an arrow, the ball cradled in his right hand, his left merely riding along as a guide, a flick of the wrist – – and string music. King Kong couldn't block that shot.

It was going to be up to me to try. I was the tallest player on our team; I was only six-two, but the other four were all about five-ten. So I had to play center. They also had two forwards who looked like they had been cut out of the same mold. They both were about my height, boney and angular. Obviously, they were from the country. One of them walked like he was stepping over corn rows. They were two tough customers.

I didn't care. I just wanted to get the game over and get to Margaret. When we were warming up, my buddy Buster grabbed me by the arm and tried to give me a little pep talk. "Listen, if you don't get the rebounds and keep that big center from scoring, we ain't got a prayer. Do you hear me?" I heard him all right. Really didn't think it would be much of a problem.

The game started, they got the ball and we went down on

defense. I tried to intimidate the big guy. He name was Crowfut I called him Crowbait. Told him he had been flying pretty high averaging nearly thirty points a game, but tonight, Mr. Crowbait, you ain't gonna get stank.

I hadn't even finished telling him what I was gonna do to him when he ran around under the basket, then flashed out toward the free-throw line, took a pass, jumped thirty-two feet straight up and flicked a shot that didn't touch anything but the bottom of the net. He was smooth as hot cane syrup.

Five minutes into the game he had scored twelve points and we were behind 15-6. Buster was our point guard, and he was scowling at me something fierce.

The coach had seen enough. He called time out. "Don't look like Culler can guard that guy," he said, "you other guys got to help." He told us what to do. Didn't help. The big guy kept pouring it on, and believe me, I was trying. I even tried to be nice to him once, to see if that would throw him off.

"Nice shot," I said .

"Kiss old Rusty," he replied.

Time out. When we got to the sideline, coach didn't talk to anyone but me. "Culler," he said, "If you don't find a way to stop that guy we're dead meat. And I'll tell you another thing. If you don't stop that guy you are going to sit next to me on the front of the bus all the way home, so I can explain the principles of defense to you."

Margaret!

In the heat of battle I had almost forgotten about her. Coach must know about it, or he wouldn't be pulling this crap. I could see her slipping away. I had to get my mind set, maybe my body would follow – "By God, ain't no Crowbait from Vienna gonna' keep me from her." Jaw set, I returned with a new purpose.

First time down court Crowbait was up to his old tricks. Ran under the basket, then cut sharply toward the free-throw line, but I was right with him. Belly-button defense. Suddenly one of those big forwards threw a screen and scraped me off. I nearly tore his shirt off getting around him, but it was too late. Crowbait had the ball, and was already leaving the floor. The scorekeeper was adding two more points. I had to block that shot! I jumped as high as I could, my left hand reaching for the rafters. Crowbait was in the air, perfectly straight, ball over his head, fingers spread behind the ball, just a wrist flick away from string music.

Looking up, I could see that stretched out as far as I could go, and jumping as high as I could, my desperate left hand was still going to be about six inches short. Margaret flashed across my brain. I hit him in the crotch as hard as I could with the back of my right hand, balled into a fist.

As soon as I hit the floor I whirled around to go for the rebound, then heard the referee's whistle. Crowbait was lying on the floor, all curled up, moaning. Everyone gathered around. No one knew what happened. We had been in a little triangle, Crowbait, the forward throwing the screen, and me. Everyone in the place had seen me jump as high as I could to block the shot. He must have been kicked somehow.

I turned to one of their forwards standing next to me. "What happened?" I asked. "Kiss old Rusty," he said. Those boys had a limited vocabulary.

After a few minutes they helped him off the floor and into the dressing room. With him gone, we began catching up. No way could they replace a player like that.

The buzzer for the half sounded, and as I trotted off the floor I looked up at the pile of girls where Margaret was sitting, and I saw her get up and walk toward the door. Good old Margaret. She sure was looking good, and she was going out in the cold to get us the back seat. And was it cold. We were having some sort of record-setting Artic blast, must have been fifteen degrees out. I had a flicker of guilt about making Margaret sit out there on that cold-as-ice bus, but she had to do it.

Old Crowbait returned for the second half, but he was but a shadow of his former self. Not only would he not scrap under the board, he wouldn't even let anyone get close to him. He tried his world-famous jump shot only three times the whole second half, but instead of being straight as an arrow and jumping three feet off the floor, he would jump about six inches and his body looked like a big "C" in the air. I blocked two of his shots and the third was an air ball. He was no longer a factor.

Those two country-boy forwards were another matter. They beat the crap out of me under the boards. I caught elbows in both eyes, nose, mouth twice, and throat. Could hardly talk. But every time I wanted to give up, I thought about Margaret out there on that bus. It gave me the strength to fight on.

Buster had a little rinky-dink jump shot, and he was killing them with it. Finally, with about five minutes to play, we caught them. Game tied. He grabbed me around the waist. "Way to hang tough, big guy," he wheezed, "don't you let 'em have anything under there, and we'll get 'em in the end."

Frankly, I didn't know if I was going to make it, Margaret or no Margaret. Those big, boney forwards were pounding the crap out of me. But fortune smiled. One of the forwards tried to drive to the basket from the top of the circle, and I managed to get a hip on him and knock him up about the third row. Took the steam out of him, by God.

We finally managed to get ahead of them by two, with fifteen seconds to play. We shot the ball and missed, it bounced high and I went up to get it, fully expecting to come down with the game-ending rebound. But that big red headed forward snatched it out of my grasp just as my fingers were closing on it. He threw it downcourt, where two of their guys were racing toward the basket. There was no one back but Buster. Good old dependable Buster. I can still see that look of panic on his face when he realized what was happening, and he wasn't going to be able to stop them, and none of us could help. He didn't. Game tied. Overtime!

Margaret! My heart bleeds for you sitting out there on that freezing bus!

They had tied it up, but it was their last gasp. Everything has its limits, even Vienna. We beat 'em by eight. Only the one forward was left that started the game for them, but he was still pounding on me when the final buzzer sounded. That was the toughest game of any kind I was ever a part of. Everyone was totally exhausted. Our team, their team, both coaches, and the fans. I looked like I had been through a meat grinder. I ran for the showers. The fun part was about to begin!

When I got to the bus everyone was shouting and singing, we were going to the state! The only place I was thinking about going was to the back of the bus. There was sweet, beautiful Margaret, sitting there smiling with purple, frozen lips. What a trooper. What had I done, Lord, to deserve this good fortune!

I sat down beside her and held her close. The coach got on, and the bus pulled out. We rode for a minute or two, and the lights went out. I turned Margaret's face up toward me and kissed her lips.

Popsickles!

Among other things, Margaret had big lips. The kind you see models having operations to get nowdays. And those big luscious lips were frozen solid! It really doesn't matter, I told myself, If I keep smooching on her they will thaw out soon enough. So I really threw myself into my work. Before long I discovered that not only were her lips frozen, but her teeth as well. Undaunted, I continued on. I knew my nice warm lips would soon thaw out her frozen ones. I gave her a sexy kiss that lasted ten minutes.

"John!"

It was the coach, calling me from the front seat. When he called me John, he was pleased. I tried to answer, but couldn't. My lips and tongue were frozen solid! Instead of my hot lips unfreezing hers, her big old lips had froze mine!

"Hmmmmm." It was all I could say.

"I been thinkin', " the coach continued, "you did such a good job on old Crowbait tonight I think I'll let you guard that forward from East Crisp who's been scoring for them. What do you think?"

"Hmmmmm."

Coach took no crap, and he instantly picked up on the fact I wasn't paying him proper respect.

"Culler, you come up here!"

I unenveloped myself from Margaret and walked up to the front of the bus.

"You sit down on that seat across from me until you can address me in a proper manner!"

I sat. But I couldn't say anything. Everything from my nose

down was numb. I tried everything I could think of to unthaw. I made big grins, I tried vibrating my lips, I flapped my tongue like a guppy. I noticed that Coach was looking at me like I had gone crazy, so I calmed it down a bit.

I was about to panic. That bus was racing over the highway at 35 miles per hour and Margaret, lovely, luscious Margaret, was waiting for me on the back seat!

Finally, after an eternity, the feeling began to come back, and when I thought I could at least emit a complete sentence, I turned to the coach – – just in time to see the city limit sign go past. We were home!

We pulled into the parking lot where the parents were waiting, but I had only one concern – – what was I going to tell Margaret? I knew she was going to be upset, I had made her sit out in that cold for an hour and a half – – for nothing!

Everyone got off the bus, and Margaret started walking toward her parents' car. I grabbed her arm. "Margaret – "

She snatched her arm away. "My sweetest dream, huh. Try my worst nightmare!"

I tried again. Again she snatched her arm away. She whirled around. "Beat it, you creep!"

She got in her Daddy's car, and I stood and watched until the tail lights disappeared in the distance. I turned and walked toward my old pickup. "Damn," I thought, "I could have sworn the creep was that guy at Furman."

Memories

There are some things in life that we all remember — our first day in school, the first real kiss, the time we learned our first born had arrived. There are also other things we remember that mean a lot, maybe not quite as important, but real moments that have a relaxed, warm place in our memories.

I grew up in a very small southern town, with plenty of free time in the summer, a lot of it spent adventuring along various creek banks and around a big old mill pond about a mile from home. It was a time when every day was exciting and every new thing an adventure, and some of the very best moments came when I had a fishing pole in my hands and each new species I encountered was something to remember.

Bluegills

I had heard about bream beds, but I was still a little shaver and had never seen one. Now I was going to be shown one by the greatest wizard of all, the man who ran the giant water-powered grist mill, the same man who stalked about the dark recesses of the mysterious place, pulling and pushing levers and holding sacks to catch the ground corn.

He was covered with a fine white powder all over his bib overalls, from his untied brogans to his grizzled face which held about a cup of meal in his three-day-old beard and eyebrows. Years later I learned he was a man to be reckoned with,

109

sporting a fiery temper and a penchant for giving anyone he saw a piece of his mind. The cussin' piece. But all he had ever given me was kindness and a soft smile. Once he even let me put my hands in the fresh ground meal. "Feel it," he said, "it's warm."

I spent a lot of time fishing in the pond by his mill and in the runoff below the water wheel, and often I saw him watching me from a window two stories up.

The day he showed me the bream bed had been one of the lesser of the better days, and I was passing the mill on my way home.

"Didn't do much good, did you?" He was sitting on the steps.

"I got some bites, but I missed them," I lied.

"Come here a minute, boy. Let me show you something," he said as he got up and started walking along the path next to the dam, right by the road. Slowly parting the covering of honeysuckle, he gazed intently into the water. "Looka there, boy. That's a bream bed, and if you drop a fat wiggler in there about daylight tomorrow morning you're going to be on to something."

It was late and the light was bad, and at first I couldn't see them. Then I saw a dark shape, then another, and another. To a small boy they were the most tremendous fish imaginable. I ran for my pole. "Wait, boy!" he said. "I'm sure your momma wants you home for supper, and these fish ain't going anywhere. Just be here early in the morning."

The most delicious time in all creation is just before sunup on a summer morning, and as I barefooted to the spot the next morning I was almost overpowered by the excitement and the sweet smell of the honeysuckle. Very carefully I parted the vines and looked into the water, but it was still too dark to see anything.

Keen with the anticipation of the battle I was sure to come, there is no way I can describe the way I felt. It was absolutely better than any Christmas morning that ever happened. I was so nervous and excited it took four tries before I could hit the worm with the hook, then the darn thing got tangled on every strand of honeysuckle within five miles. Finally it fell free, and dropped into the water with a soft "plop."

Evidently I had too much lead, because the cork sank too. "Shucks," I thought, and raised my pole to bring it in. But I didn't have too much lead, a big fat bluegill had my worm. There was a violent jerk, a tremendous sloshing and splashing in the shallow water, and I was in the middle of the fight of my life!

Finally I got him on the bank – – a tremendous bluegill, perhaps more than a pound – – and my heart was running 500 miles an hour. As I sat there admiring my prize, I heard the mill start up, and I took off to show the miller what I had done. My knees were still weak. It was a tremendous feeling. I haven't gotten over it yet!

Catfish

Spring had come and it was getting warmer every day. Occasionally a cool breeze would rustle the honeysuckle and bright green leaves just enough to remind a small boy it wasn't quite time to go barefoot yet, but the cool earth sure felt good. I was fishing below the spillway, and the roar of the water rushing through the dam drowned out every sound except those in my own head. I had been there all afternoon and was almost intoxicated by the cool, clean air and the delightful smells of early spring.

It had been almost an hour since I had a bite, and I was about to lose heart if not patience. It was a sand bottom, and I sat in the end of an old boat tied to a tree, my feet in the water. I could see the bottom almost as far out as I could reach with my pole. Fishing was easy there, as long as nothing messed with the worm. All I had to do was swing my bait out six or seven feet, then wait as the cork would slowly drift too close to the bank, whereby I would repeat the procedure.

It was now time to move the pole, because it had drifted too close, but I was entranced by the efforts of the worm, which I could see as it tried to burrow into the sand it just could reach. I had been watching the worm for several seconds when suddenly a great, dark shape materialized, slowly but definitely moving toward the worm.

It was a catfish, a catfish bigger than any I had ever seen, a giant catfish that seemed to be capable of movement by will alone, and he was slowly moving toward my bait!

For an eternity he floated toward the worm, and finally, perhaps two inches away, he stopped. I was frozen into stone. "Bite it! Bite it! Bite it!" I screamed inside, but he would not. I could have counted his whiskers, or even seen the whites of his eyes if they'd been white, but he wouldn't bite, and I dare not move.

He stayed there perhaps a minute, eyeballing the worm as I eyeballed him, predator watching prey, squared. It was a tense game with everything on the line. The worm pretended not to notice.

Then it was over. Slowly, still without noticeable movement, he slid backward into the gloom, never to be seen again.

Crappie

It was Sunday afternoon, and I was allowed to go fishing because I had stayed for church, which didn't seem too bad a price to pay – – I just couldn't pay it every week.

The mill was closed and there wasn't anyone else around, just me and all those fish I knew could hardly wait to bite, but first I had to rig up a new line because I had lost mine the day before.

I was just biting the second sinker closed when I saw an old blue Dodge coming up the road across the dam. The car pulled up to the mill and a stranger got out.

"You ain't caught 'em all, have you?" He was tall and gangly, about sixty or so, and his hair was slicked back.

"Just got here," I answered as the stranger unloaded his gear. I figured he was either a banker or a railroad man.

As he began walking toward me I knew something was very unusual. He had a pole, a tackle box, and a bucket of water. No worms, no crickets, not even a wasp nest. He sat down on a rock next to me and began unwinding his pole.

"Come here much?"

"Nearly every day, 'cept when I don't go to church on Sunday morning." I was curious. What was he gonna use for bait?

He finished unwinding his pole, then reached into his bucket and brought out a tiny minnow.

"Ain't no bass gonna bite a minner that little," I thought, but I didn't say anything. I did feel a certain superiority to the stranger though – – evidently he didn't know much about fishing.

He adjusted his cork, then flipped the little minnow up against one of the concrete pillars under the mill. Almost instantly, he jerked his pole up, and after a brief struggle brought out a white fish with black spots about the size of a big bluegill.

"I thought there would be some crappies around this old mill," he said. It was the first time I had ever heard of a crappie. I began collecting my gear.

"You leaving? Don't let me run you off."

"I forgot my minners," I lied, running for home and a piece of screen wire as fast as I could.

Bass

We all remember the bass of our lives, the biggest one we ever caught, and although mine came at a fairly early age, the years have not dimmed the memory. It was almost by accident. I was a teenager, fishing in a farm pond of about twenty acres, known as a good bream pond and an even better bull frog pond because most of it was shallow and featured logs, stumps and lily pads galore.

It was in the middle of summer, and the fish weren't doing much. Just before dark, as I was paddling in, I saw a frog jump from a log and start swimming, on top of the water, toward a small stump. Suddenly there was a terrific explosion and the frog disappeared, leaving me slack-jawed, bobbing up and down on the wake made by the big bass.

I had my bream pole and some crickets, and as fast as I could I took the line off the pole, put another on with just a hook, and tried to get the fish to take a fat cricket on top. No luck.

The next morning I had to go over to Dave's house to get my rod and reel back that he had borrowed, then go all the way to Americus to the hardware store to see if they had a top-water plug that looked like a frog. They did, at least it was painted to look like a frog on the top side, but underneath it was yellow. That was a good lesson in merchandising. It doesn't matter what it looks like to the fish, but it better look like a frog to the guy who is putting the money down.

Armed with my new bi-sexual plug (frog on top, snake belly on the bottom) I arrived at the pond that afternoon, but fished for bluegills awhile until the magic time got closer. Finally, I could stand it no longer. I paddled to within twenty feet of the stump, and made a beautiful cast. Right to the top of the stump, where the plug stuck. I tightened the line, careful to not make any racket, and fortunately the plug came free and sailed over my head. Another chance.

My next cast dropped a foot from the little stump. I waited until all the ripples died away, and gave it a little twitch. The plug went 'ploop' and the big bass took it in a heart-stopping strike.

He weighed eight pounds right on the nose, and I showed him around our only filling station for two days.

Pickerel

Junior was a black man who worked part-time for my Grandad and part-time for the railroad, and he was my hunting and fishing buddy and everlasting friend. He took up a lot of time with me, and had always lived up to everything he promised. "Someday, boy, I'm gonna take you to Miller's Lake," he said, many times.

Of course I had never seen Miller's Lake, and after anticipating the trip for so long Miller's Lake had grown in my mind to something like Lake Michigan, and the big fish in it were just frantic to bite a hook.

Actually Miller's Lake was just an old oxbow in a nearby creek, about six miles away.

Finally, just like all of Junior's promises, the big day came. We left for the big lake long before day in Junior's wagon, pulled by a trusty old mule that we called "Baptist" but could care less what we called him. We had our canes, some worms and crickets, my rod and reel, and a brand new Sears, Roebuck single shot .22 that I bought at sale for five dollars because it was all scratched up. We couldn't take the wagon all the way in because, as might be expected of such an exotic place, it was way down in the swamp and we had to walk about a quarter of a mile. My visions of Lake Michigan quickly vanished when I saw the place – – still water, five or six feet deep, and looking just like a creek except there was no current.

"This ain't it, is it, Junior?" I was clearly disappointed.

"Sho is, and it's a mighty fine place, too," he answered. "Put on something and throw it out there, see what happens."

I tied on a deep running Hawaiian Wiggler, cast it clear across to the other bank, and started reeling. Suddenly there was a mighty jerk, and I felt like I had been caught by the biggest gully-whomper in the swamp. It was a big "jack" (I've never heard anyone actually call them pickerel) and he seemed intent on destroying my $5.98 rod and reel. He did, too. I guess the thread was rotten or something, because the first two guides came off the rod, and when I looked down I discovered I was fighting the monster with just the reel and about a foot of rod. The next time I looked the third guide had gone, and the line went straight from the fish to the reel.

"That thing 'posed to do thataway?" Junior asked. I never answered because just then the fish broke off, and all I had left was about ten feet of limp line. I never did find the guides.

While I was trying to get myself together, Junior walked on down the bank and started fishing. Soon I rigged up one of the poles and started fishing with a cricket. It wasn't long before the sun began streaming into the water through the trees, and I could see literally dozens of jack slowly moving about. I was about to cry anyway, and finally I could stand it no longer. I snatched up the .22 and, holding low to account for the light difference in the water, fired at the nearest fish.

When the noise and the ripples died away, I could see the

jack slowly sinking to the bottom. Using the end of my pole, I raked him out on the bank. He was not nearly as big as he looked in the water, perhaps a pound, and he had a neat little hole right through the center of his body. Somehow his limp body wasn't the ideal portrait of a mean old jack.

"It ain't the same as catchin' one, is it , boy." I turned to see Junior staring at the hole made by the bullet.

"I shouldn'a done it," I said shamefully. And to this day, I've never shot another fish.

Striped Bass

It was an old yellow pickup, driving slow and heading right for the gas pumps. I picked up my RC so he wouldn't knock it over, stood up on the island, and continued to eat my moon pie as he pulled in.

"Howdy," he said, the word somehow managing to escape around half a Tampa Nugget that hadn't been lit in days.

He walked around the truck and into the station, but returned almost immediately followed by Red, the filling station man." – – and he ain't the biggest one I ever caught either," he was saying as he walked up to the side of the truck and rolled back a tarp.

"Goshamighty!" Red said softly as he stared into the back of the truck. There's nothing that will generate a crowd faster than two or three people exclaiming into the back of a pickup, and almost instantly the good old boys were stacked two deep. In those days, being a teenager, I was struggling to be super cool. I had a bite or two of the moon pie left, and every ounce of life in me was straining to look into that truck, but I casually finished the moonie and the RC, put the bottle down, and sauntered over.

"What is it?" someone asked. "It's a rockfish," the cigar answered, and I stood on tiptoe to get a peek. I wasn't prepared for what I saw in the back of that yellow pickup. It was the biggest fish I had ever seen, probably near forty pounds, lying from the front of the bed almost to the tailgate, with a slightly yellow cast and dim lines running the length of his body. I can still remember the glazed-over eyes almost as big as quarters.

"...caught him over to the river," the cigar was saying, "...no, got him on cut bait right up in the rocks,...yeah, boy, he shore did pull....I guess it took about fifteen minutes..."

To a boy who thought a ten-pound largemouth was the biggest fish in the world, the striper was quite a sight. Before the cigar quit talking I was making mental plans on how I could get to the river, but it was years later and many miles away before I caught my first striper.

Trout

When I was about twelve I went to visit my aunt in Rosman, North Carolina, up in the mountains. She had promised to take me trout fishing, and sure enough, my aunt, uncle and I left early one morning in a jeep.

That day turned out to be a first for me in many ways. It was the first time I had ever been in the mountains, fished with a spinning rod, or put my feet in ice water.

My uncle handed me a rod, complete with a tiny spinner with two blades. My mind was full of a thousand questions.

He showed me how to use the spinning rod. I tried a few casts, and was convinced there was nothing to it. "You have to learn how to wade in a trout stream," he was telling me, but I was so eager to give it a try I could hardly hear him.

He gave me a five-minute sermon of what to do and how to do it, and finished by telling me to watch him, "until you learn what you are doing." I watched intently as he waded into the swift, knee-deep water, slipped, got a panic stricken look on his face, and fell down. His waders filled up with ice water.

I didn't know my uncle that well then, and I tried not to laugh, but just couldn't help it. He called me a "little dirty name," then we all went fishing. I had never walked in fast water before, and I was surprised not only at how cold it was, but how strong. But the spinning rod was easy to master, and soon I caught my first trout. He was small, but he really put up a fight. I also learned that trout don't feel like other fish, but are wiggly and slick, almost like an eel.

Before the day was over I caught five or six more, and so did my uncle, all about the same size. I saw my uncle hook one big one, probably several pounds, but he threw the spinner on the first jump, and my uncle said some words I had never heard before.

It was a day I'll always remember, but it wasn't because the fish were big. It was the crisp green of the trees, the clear, strong, cold water; the clean smell everything had, the adventure that waited behind every bend in the river. I go back every year. The trout are the same size, but the other values there become more and more pleasurable as the years pass.

Angels at No-Name Creek

*At one time all hunters and fishermen
went to heaven, but that's no longer true.
In fact, it's getting extremely crowded
down below. Some folks have been there
months and have never even seen a fire!*

*T*he sign said "No-Name Creek." Just my kind of place.
Traveling about the state I had crossed old "No-Name"
several times, a beautiful old black-water creek that just
had to be fine redbreast country.

One day I saw the sign and began thinking how much fun
it would be to catch some fish and photograph them, then
when the guys at the office asked where I caught them I could
say, "No-Name Creek." I figured it would make everyone who
asked mad. I had to be back that way on Friday, so proper plans
were made.

That Friday I got there about three in the afternoon, and I
was ready. I had a bream-buster, about a hundred crickets and
a can of real worms. The kind you dig yourself in the cowlot
and not the store-bought kind. I don't mind telling you it was
a fine group of worms, too. Each one had to be wrestled down

120

individually before he would stay in the can.

I had long before learned that big worms like this always work better, because when a fish can find himself one of these he doesn't have to eat again for a month, and of course, that saves a lot of swimming around. I remember that can held one big fellow I caught when he was crawling around under a tree eating acorns.

I had loaded up with pole, bait, tackle box, croker sack, two corncob pipes and about a half-pound of a special tobacco mixture. The tobacco mix I did myself and I called it "Old 37," because it was the thirty-seventh mix I had tried before I got one I liked.

Since I'm sure some of you fine folks are pipe smokers, perhaps we should pause in the midst of this little story and let me tell you about the tobacco. I'm sure you will like it too.

I hate pipes that keep going out. You ever notice how many times a fellow who smokes a pipe has to keep lighting it? Plenty. But you don't have to worry about this mixture going out.  To every quarter-pound of tobacco (it doesn't matter which kind) add a pinch or two of shaving from a pencil sharpener, a tablespoon of grits which have been soaked in kerosene overnight, six drops of honey, a tablespoon of cane syrup and the powder from one high-brass shotgun shell. Add a little nutmeg if you like a sweet aroma, mix well, put in a dark place and let it work for about a week. It packs nice, smokes sweet and if you have made it right, goes out only when you have about an inch of stem left in your teeth.

Anyway, I walked down the bank a little way to get away from the bridge, found a likely spot, dropped a worm in and settled back. The fish weren't doing much. I would like to lie about It, but I just can t lie to a reader. The afternoon sort of dragged on, and I moved several times, but the fishing was slow. Only one incident of note occurred. About five o'clock a really good-looking young woman came down the opposite bank, stopped directly across the creek from me (must be the sweet smelling pipe, I thought) and started fishing under a log. Just about as fast as she could pull 'em, she caught three big redbreasts. While she was baiting up to go after the next one, I decided to break the ice by using an introduction given to me by Mike Creel. I should have thought first.

"My name be John. What might'en be yourn?" I said in a loud voice. Mike said it had never failed. It didn't this time either. Without a word she rolled the line around her pole and left. I couldn't believe it. Left a hot fishing spot too.

A few minutes later, I was nearly asleep when I heard sort of a shuffling noise behind me. I tried to ignore it, but it grew louder. Finally, fearful of being eaten by a giant snake, I turned around. Friends, you may not believe what I am going to tell you, but right behind me were two of the strangest looking characters I have ever seen. They looked like they stepped out of the last century. Bloodshot eyes, sleeves and pants rolled up, one wore suspenders, the other barefoot, and to make the whole scene even more unbelievable, they were riding three giant snapping turtles!

"Howdy," the nearest one said. "I'm Austin and this here is Ed. We's angels, and we is on a special mission."

Friends, I couldn't believe what I was seeing, but one of them had an axe so I figured I had better be careful.

"You don't look like any angels I've ever seen," I answered, trying to think of any angels I had seen, but couldn't think of a single one.

Austin spoke. "Well, we ain't angels from Heaven, we's

angels from down there," he pointed toward the ground. "Guess we do look a little different."

"What are you doing here, then? Yau'll live down here on No-Name Creek?"

"Heck, no," he said. "To make a long story short, things are gittin' too crowded down there in Hell. We've been sent up here to see if we can change the ways of some people and stop the overcrowding situation. It's so bad, we've got folks down there nigh on to ten years that ain't even had their hair singed yet!"

"Are there any kind of special folks that you have been getting a lot of?"

"Democrats. Wall to wall Democrats. You won't believe the politicians we've been gittin' lately. And lawyers. And, if a lawyer ever turned politician, we would get him for sure. For awhile there, we thought politicians might challenge bankers for number one, but that was a joke. Every banker who ever lived eventually moved in with us."

"Don't forget doctors," Ed said. "Lord yes. Ever since greed got popular, we been gettin' doctors. And dentists, too."

I wasn't about to ask him about book publishers. Or writers.

"Well," I ventured, trying to find a ray of sunshine, "at least you don't get many hunters and fishermen, even if they are politicians."

They looked at each other very sadly, then in tearful tones they related heart-rending stories of shooting over the limit, poaching, duck baiting, cussing, willful lying, blowing up fish and other terrible things.

Ed said that almost all hunters and fishermen went to Heaven a few years ago, but now it was about half and half.

"That's why we's here," Austin said, "we's gittin' too many people we don't need. It's gotta stop!"

I asked them how long they had been on earth, and was told they had been here five years, working solely on hunters and fishermen, and had not been able to influence a single one. "We worked on one fellow from up around Pittsburgh for more'n three months, and thought he was going to make it, then he had that accident," Austin related.

"Accident?"

"Yeah. He was a fly fisherman, and he was fishing in a little creek by the road, when he hooked a Greyhound Bus on his backcast. The language that man used! All our work went right down the drain."

"What happened to the bus?"

"It didn't make but one run," Ed giggled, "but that one was long and strong. You could say it was sustained. Ran all his backing off then jerked the guts right out of his reel. You know how they like to use those strong leaders up there!"

I asked about the turtles, and was told they rode them cause they moved slow, "and we don't want to miss anyone." Said they didn't get many dogs messing with them either.

"What about you," Austin asked. "Are you a pretty decent fellow?"

"I guess I am," I beamed. "Why, just awhile ago the best looking girl you ever saw came up on the other side of the creek, took one look at me and tried her best to get me to let her come over here. I told here to get out of here and leave me alone."

The two angels exchanged glances.

Ed took out a book and searched in it for a moment. "He's gonna get spot number five hundred eighty-nine million six hundred and nine." With that, they shuffled on down the creek.

Other Values

It ain't always what you kill that matters, there are all kinds of things to be found on a hunt. Unfortunately, Clancy never spent much time discovering other values.

I t was a beautiful November day. Like all beautiful days in the south in fall, this one had all the required parts. Blue sky, gold and red leaves, crisp, cool air and for the most part, happy people.

The only person that wasn't happy was Clancy, but that wasn't too unusual because there were very few days when Clancy was happy, no matter what month it was.

Clancy's particular cause for unhappiness this day was a little patch of woods that was suspected to harbor two or three big bucks in the "grandpappy" category, and which, even after an hour of drawing plans of attack on the ground, was still too big to drive effectively with the five people we had on hand.

"It's all right, Clancy," I volunteered, "you don't know for sure there are any bucks in that place. Besides, there are plenty of other places we can drive with what we got."

"Ain't Mr. Cleveland said he saw a buck run in there off the road three times this month? And you know yourself we saw that deer slipping through those trees last year." He sounded exactly like a man who knew what he was talking about. "'Sides, ain't nowhere else they could be. We ain't jumped nothin' to speak of any-where else 'round here lately." I had to admit he was right, but the fact remained we didn't have enough people to stand the place.

Clancy was a great guy, but boy was he hardheaded. We all knew it would be useless to suggest that we stand half-way and hope someone got a shot.

"Ain't no use doin' nothin' if we ain't gonna do it right," was Clancy's favorite piece of advice. "Now think about it for a minute," he'd say, "if you were a buck, would you run where there was somebody or where there wasn't somebody?" None of us wanted to listen to all of that crap, we had heard it before.

We finally gave up and decided to drive a small section of woods down the road, a spot we hunted about once a week with the same negative results, unless you count that spike that Steve got the first week of October.

When we drove up to the intersection where the two little dirt roads crossed, there was a new Buick parked there, contain-ing four fellows dressed for hunting. Their average age was about eighty, and they were laughing and carrying on like they were having the biggest time of their life. The idea hit me and Clancy at the same time – –"If they would hunt with us, we could make the drive where the big bucks are!"

Clancy whipped the dog wagon over to the side. The four men got out to look at the hounds, and I could see Clancy sizing them up. They were a bunch of old gaffers all right, but they looked like they could do the job. They sure did seem to be happy about everything, anyway.

Clancy must have been satisfied. "How would yau'll like to hunt with us?" he asked. "We got this little place up the road where we believe we could do some good, but we ain't got enough standers."

Their eyes lit up. "Sure, sure. We would be delighted, young man. We appreciate the invitation." It was Clancy's eyes that lit up then, and we piled back on the truck and turned around. Clancy was plenty excited.

"We're gonna git a big 'un today!" he kept saying over and over. His demeanor was similar to that of a man on the trail of a big pot of gold.

Clancy drew a simple plan in the dirt. He would put us all on a stand, then he would take the dogs around to the other side and drive right through the middle of the place. If there was a buck in there, we would have him.

After we took our stands, I could see one of the old fellows on the stand next to me, just down the road a piece. Clancy had no sooner got out of sight when the old guy was joined by one of his friends, who I assumed, had been placed on the other side of him. They were still there, laughing and talking, twenty minutes later when Clancy started the drive.

Old Clance was whooping and hollering for all he was worth, and pretty soon one of the hounds jumped and let the music roll. He was soon joined by the whole pack, and deer, hounds and Clancy swept up through the woods, headed straight for me.

At first I didn't see anything, then I did! A big rascal, running like a racking horse, head high, sun reflecting off a gigantic rack of polished antlers. Deer hunters everywhere will tell you there is no other sight like it. Suddenly he swerved to the left and went behind a thicket. I lost him for a moment, and when I saw him again he was running straight toward the two old fellows who were still standing in the road.

Laughing and talking a moment before, now they stood staring at the big buck bearing down on them.

I expected them to react any second, but they stood stock still, their guns cradled in their arms. The deer jumped in the road not ten steps from the two, stared at them for a brief second, then disappeared forever in the woods beyond. They never moved.

I couldn't believe it, and neither could Clancy, who came running up, red faced and out of breath. He had seen the whole thing too, and it was incredible, neither of the men had made any attempt to shoot!

"What's the matter," Clancy half screamed. "Why didn't you shoot?"

"Shoot? Why, we never shoot," one of the old fellows said with a smile. "But it was a fantastic sight, wasn't it?"

I thought Clancy was going to die. "You mean you let us go through all this and you messed up our hunt and all you got to say is how exciting it was?"

The old fellow was perplexed. "You never asked us to shoot anything," he said. "You asked us if we wanted to hunt with you. We agreed, because we all love to hunt. But we quit shooting years ago. If we had killed that deer, we would have had to drag him out of the woods, skin him out, cut him up, and go through the hassle of dividing the meat, then doing something with it when we got home. We're too old to do all that, so we just enjoy the other benefits of the hunt without any of the work."

"You came out here to not shoot deer?" Clancy was livid. "I have a better suggestion for you. Why don't all of you old fuddy-duds go down in the swamp somewhere and not shoot some squirrels, then yau'll go out to Arkansas and not shoot some ducks – – and stay out of our way!"

With that, he stomped off toward the truck. It would take us two hours to round up all the hounds.

Later Clancy finally got to where he would laugh about the

129

incident, and he even admitted that even he got a lot out of hunting that couldn't be measured by the weight of the game bag.

Are Women Human?

Women are like us in many ways,
but then, there are a lot of ways they
don't resemble us at all. Are they really
another species that have learned to fill a
biological role in our lives? Maybe there
is a test that could be given.

I had a special friend when I was growing up. He lived down the street a few houses from me and was three or four years younger than I was. His name was Timothy Prince and he was a real intellectual.

Timothy had an I. Q. of about 200, but he wasn't a particularly good student. The reason was, the teacher would be on page 57, but Timothy would be on page 213, or possibly page 57 of the book they had just finished, or maybe even page 57 of the book he had decided to write on the subject.

Most of the guys avoided Timothy, not that he would ever notice, but he just wasn't into the same things that other 14-year-old boys were. But I liked Timothy, and he liked me. I guess it was because I was older that he trusted me, I don't know. Timothy was always asking weird questions that made you think. Like, "If we can remember the past, why can't we remember the future?" If you responded that it was because we hadn't lived it yet, he would be waiting for that answer like a tiger in the weeds. When you talked to old Timothy you had better be sharp.

One summer afternoon I was mowing the grass when Timothy showed up. Always alert for an excuse to quit, we sat down on the grass. We sort of just sat there for a few minutes, then Timothy said, "I have been thinking about it a good bit, and I have decided that girls, meaning women, the female, is not a member of the human race."

Now I had sense enough to know that Timothy was at a bad age, that he probably felt uncomfortable around girls and that he was undoubtedly trying to sort it all out in his mind. I also knew that he never made snap decisions – – this was something he had been working on for awhile.

Timothy continued. "Since all arguments should be based on facts, let's start with one. Fact: we are human. Meaning males. Boys are definitely human. Fact number two: to be considered human, any other creature must resemble known humans. They must think like humans, act like humans, eat like humans, and look like humans. Girls do none of these."

He paused, waiting in the weeds.

"But Timothy," I began, " girls are just the female version of boys. They do resemble us, I mean, they have two arms and legs and stand upright like us. Their differences are just biological, since they are female and we are male."

"I know there are a lot of similarities," said Timothy, " but we have similarities with other creatures too, such as gorillas, and we certainly do not consider them human. I have been trying to think like a girl. I cannot do it. They are not interested in anything that we are, and they don't think about things the same way that we do.

"I know they are like us in some ways; for instance, they feel pain; they are sad when a pet dies, like we are; and they do have strong emotions toward certain other people; but even dogs feel pain, and have emotions. So that's not proof. I think females are another species entirely, that they somehow learned to fulfill the biological female role and hung on to a good thing."

There was a pause while both of us thought on it a bit.

He continued. "Just the other day I was watching my mother. Every time dad wants to lie on the couch and watch a ball game, mother does everything she can to get him moving again. She doesn't seem to care what he does, as long as he is doing something. Wash the car, mow the lawn, paint the fence. I think that behavior is a response to a primeval survival mode that was necessary back in cave man days but has long since passed its time.

"Back then, if the male was lounging about the cave, he wasn't out getting something for supper. And if he didn't get something for supper, there wasn't going to be any, because they certainly didn't have a way to keep anything. So the woman who could nag and browbeat the best lived to pass on her genes, while the good old gals who went with the flow soon died out."

He was starting to roll. "Now how many girls do you know that can read a road map? Granted, a few can, but not many. Now don't you think ——"

When he stopped, I looked up, and coming around the

corner on her bicycle was Rebecca Primrose. Rebecca was Margaret Primrose's little sister. You probably know about Margaret by now. Margaret was the prettiest, sexiest, most wonderful girl in Lee County High School. If Margaret was a ten, not another girl in the whole school would score above a six. Margaret was every red-blooded American boy's dream. Lord! Margaret was fine!

The problem was Margaret was too fine for any boy in school. She was going steady with a junior in college, a rich boy who played tight end on the Furman football team. He thought he was hot stuff, and so did Margaret. However, the tight end was working under a certain disadvantage; that was that Furman University wasn't in South Georgia. So I had been hanging around Margaret's house a good bit, trying to give her a chance to make a wonderful discovery. She was sweet and flirty, but so far had failed to recognize the potential.

Rebecca was about three years younger than Margaret. She must have been about fourteen or so. Rebecca was Margaret in miniature. She wasn't there yet, but she was a real comer, you could tell.

She had long brown hair that hung down over her shoulders in waves, like a model. A beautiful smile, a mischievous gleam in her eye, and beautiful suntanned legs. Yessir, a real comer.

The Primrose girls both had something in common. They had been born knowing how to flirt. Margaret had refined it to a science by the time she was eight or so, but Rebecca had it down by the time she was five. Maybe it was because second children have to try harder, I don't know.

Rebecca saw us sitting there on the grass and a smile spread across her face. I had learned all of Rebecca's little tricks from hanging around Margaret's house so much, and I was looking forward to her attack. And I knew it was going to be an attack. She leaned her bicycle against a tree, and started walking toward us.

"Beat it, little girl. This is man talk over here," I said.

We were sitting on the grass with our arms on top of our knees. Rebecca walked behind me, got down on her knees, and put her arms around my neck. Her face pushed hard up against mine. She was having a great time. "You better get out of here and stop that before your mama sees you," I warned her. She giggled and walked around in front of us, and looked down at me with a sly little expression on her beautiful 14-year-old face.

"H..e..y, I..o..h..n," she said, dragging it out. She was wearing a tank top and a pair of short white shorts. She stared down at me for a few seconds; then slowly, very slowly, like a lizard eyeing a bug, she turned her face toward poor Timothy. Chronologically, they were about the same age. Biologically, Timothy wasn't in the same universe. "Hello, T..i..m..o..t..h..y," she cooed. I swear, the Timothy part took twenty seconds to get out of her mouth.

This girl had a pair of the most beautiful eyes there has ever been. I don't care if they were only fourteen years old. She turned twenty thousand volts of pure girl power right in Timothy's face, and held it there. Timothy melted like a hot candle. All the way down into his shoes.

Poor Timothy tried to say something, got all balled up, and just mumbled. He was as red as a South Georgia sundown.

She watched him until she was sure she had utterly destroyed him, then turned back to me. "Well, it doesn't look like there will be any fun around here with you two." I'm sure she was feeling proud of herself, being able to destroy a real smart guy with just a look. "I guess I might as well go now," she laughed, and tripped toward her bike.

She couldn't resist one last shot." When are you going to stop panting around my sister and move into the first team?" she said to me, "I've got twice as much of anything she's got!"

"Beat it, brat." I wanted to keep her in her place. "Come back in about five years when you grow up!" She pedaled down the street, and I turned back to Timothy. He looked like a pod of dried out Devil's snuff.

"Timothy, you let that little girl destroy you! You must be sweet on her or something. What is it? Is that the truth? You're sweet on her, aren't you! Say it!" He wouldn't say anything, just sat there in a comatose state.

"Well, I guess that ends the argument. It certainly proves that girls are human. Only a girl could have done what she did to you. A gorilla couldn't have done it, neither could a chimp. I'm glad we got it resolved."

I had to go. It was almost supper time, and I didn't want to be late. I liked to get finished so I could get on over to Margaret's. One day, I thought, something will happen to that tight end, and I'm gonna be Margaret's safety net!

137

*Technology is making rapid strides
down at the police department, but if your
town has one of these you are in big trouble!
It may not be too late to clean up your act,
but you better hurry!*

My wife and teen-age daughter decided to drive down to Columbus, Georgia for the week-end and visit my wife's mother. It was o.k. by me; I could use a quiet week-end of Braves baseball and an occasional steak, not to mention being my own boss for a day or two.

They left Friday afternoon and everything went great until about Bull-bat time, when I had just settled in for the first pitch with a two-pound steak, a pitcher of milk straight from the cow, and some light bread.

I heard the front door slam. It was Clancy, and he had a big bottle of something dark under his arm.

"Look what I brought you, boy," he proudly held out the bottle. "It's some twisted wine, the first I ever made, and I wanted you to share it with me."

I wasn't surprised, because I knew Clancy had been fooling

around trying to make wine. He certainly had spirit making in his genes, his Grandpa and Pa had been famous back in Georgia as top moonshiners in the old days.

"Twisted wine? I never heard of twisted wine. I didn't know there was such a thing."

"There is now," insisted Clancy. In case you don't know about moonshine, twisted whiskey is made by first making whiskey, then pouring it back in the still and running it through again. The second time around the alcohol content skyrockets and there is even less of anything good in it. You don't have as much whiskey as you start out with, but it's much more potent. Some of the old boys would run it through three or four times, and have something you could spill on the car seat and it would eat all the way to the ground, asphalt and all. But I had never heard of twisted wine.

"I just took what I got the first time and made it all over again," he explained. "Two or three times."

He went on to explain that he wouldn't be able to stay and help me drink it, as his wife was in the car and they were headed out to hear some chamber music at the church.

Clancy left, and I sat the bottle on the kitchen table and got back to the game, just in time to hear the announcement. Rain delay. Crap! Sanford and Son came on. I sat there depressed, eating my steak and staring at Clancy's wine. I certainly wasn't going to drink any of it.

Took a little nap. Woke up and watched "This Week

139

in Baseball." Then Sheriff Andy Taylor and Barney came on. Old Barn is my favorite, but I had seen that episode three times. Still raining in Atlanta. I was getting real bored.

Old bottle of wine still sitting there.

"I wonder if Clancy really can make twisted wine?"

The bottle didn't do nothing. Just sat there waiting.

"Well, hell, might as well try just a little taste. That can't do any harm," I rationalized as I reached for a glass. I have to tell you, it wasn't too bad. Not like drinking kerosene or something. But it did have a certain presence. I put an ice cube in it, and that smoothed it out some. I drank another glass.

The stuff sort of grew on you. I didn't even put any ice in the third glass, but I did notice it was sure getting hot in there. Checked the stove. Nope. Wasn't on.

The doorbell rang. Anyone I knew would have just come on in, must be a salesman.

I opened the door, and there stood a tall guy, dressed like Wyatt Earp. Cowboy hat and all. Hard eyes and thin lips. Wearing a big badge. "I'm the Right Reverend Harold Stillwell, with the police. I'd like to talk to you, Mr. Culler. Seems you are in a certain amount of trouble. May I come in?"

"Why sure, come on in. I was just having a glass of wine. Won't you join me?"

"Hardly." He said, kind of cold. We walked back to the kitchen and sat down.

"I don't know how to address you, sir." I was as polite as could be to this long, tall stranger. "Are you Rev. Stillwell, like the Rev. Mr. Jesse Jackson, or Officer Stillwell, like Officer Ding Dong of the Royal Mounted Police?"

"If I were you, I would keep a civil tongue in my head," he said. "You may address me as Officer Stillwell."

He explained he was with the Camden City Police, The Mind Division. "The Mind Division?" I had never heard of such a thing.

"I knew I would have to explain it to you," he said in a very exasperated manner. "You may know that crime technology has been making rapid advancement. A few years ago the equipment was developed that allowed police officers to read the thoughts of certain criminals, therefore making it possible to prevent many crimes before they occur. We have been equipped with this technology at the department for several years, and it's my job to keep up with whose minds is wondering where, and to nip trouble in the bud."

He looked at me with jaundiced eye. "That's why I'm here. Your mind has been wondering to places it doesn't belong." And another thing, he continued, he didn't think it was much of an ambition just to want to be a dirty old man, like I did. "That's not much ambition for a person who had a Christian raisin' and an eighth-grade education."

This guy was starting to get under my skin. "What do you mean, an eighth-grade education! I have you know I graduated from high school! In fact, I went thirteen years! You better get your facts straight!"

"You might have gone thirteen years, but only eight years took. The rest was a waste of time."

I'll have to admit, he had me there.

He looked me in the eye with a steely stare. "I've been watching your thought patterns for several years. Your mind didn't wander much. Didn't have enough power to get you in any trouble. Just wandered out to the sidewalk and back. Then last fall you fell in the creek. Do you remember that?"

I did remember it. I was squirrel hunting, and I tried to walk across that old log and fell in the creek.

"The best we can figure down at the station is when your mind fell in the creek, it was below the sewage effluent, and there was a lot of nutrients in the water. Your mind must have picked up some strength, because the next thing we knew it had wandered down the street and got all over Mr. Adams' new bride, Doris Jean. The things your mind did to that young woman were scandalous, shameful, and disgusting!"

"Oh, you mean the part with the whipped cream and rubber sheet?"

"What whipped cream?" He began looking through his notes.

"Heck, man. That was the best part."

"I don't seem to have that. Tell me about it. Every detail," he ordered.

"I ain't tellin' you nothin. If you ain't got it, you ain't got it."
He must have thought I was a fool.

While he was shufflin' through his notes I poured him a
glass of wine. "You sure seem to be wound up awful tight, Officer
Stillwell, why don't you have a glass of wine and relax a little."

"Well," he glanced at the clock, "I guess it is after nine. Just
a little sip."

"This wine is a little rough at first, want me to put some ice
in it?"

Said he didn't want any ice, he liked to
take his drinks neat. And he did. I poured him
another. Had another myself.

Soon Clancy's best began to warm him
up, and he started talking about his job, and
some of the things he had seen on various
folks minds. "The lawyers are the worst," he
told me. "They are always thinking up dirty little things. Ain't just sex stuff either. They try
to think up ways to get money out of people
without having to do anything for it."

"I'm glad to know you are on the job,"
I told him, and meant it.

"Doctors are no trouble, they think
about certain nurses sometime, but that's
natural. Mostly, they are so tired when
they get home their minds ain't got enough
energy to wander out the front door."

I poured him another glass of Clancy's
finest.

"What about some of these bad characters around town, the ones that get
gossiped about so much," I asked. "Oh
they are a piece of cake," he said. "They go
and do it, don't just dream about it. They
are the easiest ones for my division."

He took off his vest and
unbuttoned his shirt. "Shore is
hot in here, brother Culler." I had

experienced that very same feeling. His eyes got steely again. "I want you to quit letting your mind wonder on that new third-grade school teacher we got, that Nellie whats-her-name. You been thinkin' some awful evil things about that girl!"

I tried to remember. I knew the young lady in question, but I couldn't remember ever giving her a thought. "But the worst of all," he continued, "is the Chief's secretary, Pam Parker. You aught to be ashamed of yourself. That little vision of yau'll going to Atlanta was a disgrace! Ain't no way that nice lady could twist her back around like that!"

Now I didn't know Pam Parker, but I knew what was happening. "Hold it," I gave him my own steely stare. "That ain't my mind wondering on them women – it's yours!"

He sat back in his chair and looked surprised, then sad. "Yes, I guess it is mine – – but you ain't gonna tell anybody are you?"

I felt kinda bad about it, after all, he didn't mean no harm, and he seemed to be a pretty nice guy.

Suddenly, he brightened up. "Do you know I can recite Lincoln's Gettysburg address?" The last thing I wanted to hear was Lincoln's Gettysburg address. But he stood up where he was and gave me the benefit of it, and did a fine job, too. I told him it might sound better if he stood up on the chair and gave it, and he did. Then he stood on the table and gave it, and did another fine job.

We both had another glass of Clancy's award-winning wine.

The last thing I remember of that evening was The Right Reverend Stillwell standing in the sink, clad only in his drawers, cowboy hat and boots, holding a broom for a microphone, singing the national anthem.

I remember thinking right before I passed out that I was glad they didn't have a Mind Police Swat Team, because there would be some folks around here that would really be in big trouble.